Wild Wild Widow

EMMA JAY

Copyright © 2022 by Emma Jay

All rights reserved.

No part of this book may be reproduced in any form or by any electronic or mechanical means, including information storage and retrieval systems, without written permission from the author, except for the use of brief quotations in a book review.

❦ Created with Vellum

CHAPTER
One

Rebecca Chatham took her seat in the box overlooking the stage at the opera house. Murmurs from the elite of San Francisco society rippled through the room and she saw more than one gaze turn away when she made eye contact. Accustomed to the treatment, she lifted her chin and cast a small smile to her escort. Neville Frost was younger than her by three or four years, and an interesting mix of sophistication and anxiety. He'd been taught all the niceties of society but didn't appear to have put them to use.

He sat beside her on a velvet seat in his family's box, closer than was strictly proper, but she understood his intent. This was no courtship leading to marriage. He planned to ask her to be his mistress.

She'd only been widowed eight months, and if she cared what society thought, that length of time would give her pause. She'd loved her wild, wicked husband, but she missed the touch of a man. Her gaze dropped to Neville's hands—long-fingered, slim, young. He would be gentle. If he was old and ill-favored, would she still consider it? Perhaps, if it meant escaping her father's house, more confining now that she'd known freedom.

The lights dimmed, and he edged closer. They had the box to themselves this evening. She didn't move away, and when he stroked the soft skin above her glove, heat flashed through her. She'd so missed this, the gentle caresses, the personal touches. Had she been touched since Nathan died? No, by no other than her maid. Not even her father had so much as placed a comforting hand on her shoulder as she grieved the loss of her husband.

Neville's breathing changed, grew deeper, and a giggle bubbled inside her. Would the people in the next box be able to hear him? They certainly couldn't see him, as he bent his head toward her bare throat. She angled her head in invitation, and he pressed a soft kiss to the curve of her neck. Oh, yes. Not too wet, almost timid. Delicious. She let her eyes drift shut as his hand slid up her arm to the sleeve of her gown.

"So soft," he murmured. "So lovely." His touch shifted to the back of her neck, where he brushed his thumb back and forth beneath her hairline, over her spine.

She was mistaken. He was not inexperienced, not if he could make her feel like this. She knew she should be thinking about setting ground rules—she'd never been a mistress before, but understood it was a business arrangement—but her body was taking over, her breath coming faster, her nipples beading, her breasts aching. She wanted his mouth on her skin, but he only continued that caress, making her insane with longing.

And then, when the lights dimmed just a bit more to simulate evening on the stage, he kissed her, almost gentlemanly, if not for the fact that they were in a public place. A whimper escaped her, and she closed her gloved hand around his as he withdrew.

Dark eyes hooded, he traced the low-cut neckline of her gown, then eased her further into the shadows and dipped his head to taste her skin. With a shaking hand, he cupped her breast beneath the fabric, slipping it free and lifting it toward his mouth.

His warm lips had just closed over her nipple when the lights came up and a screech of disgust echoed throughout the opera house. Rebecca opened her eyes to meet the gaze of Elspeth Frost, Neville's sister, who stared from her brother to Rebecca's naked breasts.

Oh, dear.

———

Rebecca kept her spine straight as she sat on the settee in her father's study. She refused to acknowledge the frisson of fear as she faced him across his massive desk. His glower was more intimidating than when she'd said she'd marry Nathan Chatham, more intimidating than when she'd come to him after her husband had been killed in a duel and had left her destitute. While she'd caused more than one scandal as Mrs. Nathan Chatham, she hadn't been under her father's roof. This latest debacle reflected badly on him. Over the past few hours, she had been mentally composing what he would say to her.

Her fingers itched to pluck at her skirt, but she willed them still. Her father held her gaze for a long time, as if willing her to drop hers in a gesture of subservience, but she refused.

"Daughter, you have shamed me for the last time."

Despite her best efforts, she couldn't stop the flush that crept up her throat. Neville's sister had grabbed him by his ear and dragged him away, leaving Rebecca bare to the people who poked their heads into the box to see why Elspeth was screaming.

"I'm going to take into account that your husband let you run wild during your marriage. Of course you see where that got him —and you. You found yourself homeless, unwelcome by the best people in society. The only purpose young Frost had in escorting you last night was for the nefarious purposes you experienced." He took a deep breath and dropped his gaze, his own face coloring. Then he met her gaze again, his expression devoid of any fatherly affection. Of course, when had there been any? "In order to remove your influence from your sisters, I'm sending you to Gabriel and Beatrice."

She sucked in the protest before it exploded from her lips. Her brother Gabriel was more grim than her father, and his wife Beatrice was the most uptight woman Rebecca knew, and she had met her fair share in San Francisco society. Worse, her brother's ranch was in Central California, so far away from the excitement of San Francisco. She didn't even own any clothes suitable for living on a ranch—her riding habits were more for show than function. Perhaps she could still convince Neville she would make a suitable mistress and he could put her up in an apartment. She would do anything he wanted if it meant she didn't have to go live on a ranch.

A cold smile spread across her father's face. "I've already sent him a telegram, and he's agreed. Your maid is packing your things."

For a moment, she hoped he meant Neville, but of course he didn't.

"You leave today." He rose and walked out of the study before her mind could form an argument.

———

Good heavens, California was, well, empty once one left San Francisco. Rebecca focused her gaze out the train window and watched the rolling brown hills, occasionally broken by fences, sometimes dotted with trees, sometimes with horses, and a few cattle. All of this brownness left her with a sense of isolation. She sat back on her seat—at least her father saw to it that she traveled comfortably—and willed herself not to cry.

No more balls, no more theater, no more riding in the park to see and be seen. Of course, she'd been limited in these activities since she was still technically in mourning, but she'd enjoyed them so when she'd been married, and had looked forward to resuming them in a few months' time.

Her father had given no indication of when, if ever, she'd be allowed to return home, and she hated to admit to the fear that had prevented her from asking.

Why, oh, why had she let Neville take such liberties before ensuring he could take care of her?

The trip to the southern end of the Salinas River Valley was only a day, but it was so different from home—the only home she'd known—it may as well have been weeks away. The train pulled to a halt in front of a wooden depot so new the boards hadn't been painted. Dust swirled on the other side of the train, and when she took a deep breath, ready to disembark and find her brother, she almost choked with the dust and heat.

What had her father exiled her to? By the time she reached the door of the train, her hair was damp with perspiration, and she questioned her decision to wear her wool traveling suit. Of course, in San Francisco, wool was perfectly suitable. Here, none of her clothing would be. She tightened her grip on her satchel and stepped onto the platform.

She glanced around, looking for her brother. She hadn't seen him in six years, so wasn't sure she'd recognize him right away. Surely he would be a man alone. Beatrice wouldn't accompany him. But no man approached her, and the ones who remained were unfamiliar.

Very few of her fellow passengers disembarked, so after a few moments, she and her maid were alone on the platform, with her trunks piled nearby. The conductor tipped his hat and got back on the train, which chugged away.

"Let's at least go in out of the heat," Rebecca said at last. She felt bad for her maid, Sonia, who had done nothing to be exiled, sent away from her family for an indeterminate length of time.

The building smelled of fresh-cut lumber, the scent stirred up by the whirring fan in the corner.

"Miss, you don't want to leave your things out on the platform there," the man said from behind the grate.

"Is there someone who can help me move them?"

"No, ma'am, I'm all alone here today."

"May I leave this here?" She set her satchel on the bench by the door.

"I'll keep an eye on it."

Reaching up, she removed the pins from her hat, which was listing anyway, and so hot, and impractical against the beating sun. She set it on top of the satchel, then removed her jacket, dropped it on top of all, and strode out to get her own damned luggage.

She'd lifted the end of the second trunk to drag it inside when a man cleared his throat.

She shoved her hair out of her face and looked up at the lean, laconic cowboy mounting the platform.

"Can I give you a hand with that?"

Half a dozen men just like him had walked on by ignoring her, and between their rudeness and the heat, her patience was at an end. "I can do it."

"One of those, are you?" He stopped beside her, so his dusty boots and pants were all she saw as she bent over the heavy trunk.

She straightened. He was closer than she realized, and her skirts brushed his boots as she looked up into his brown eyes, shaded by a brown cowboy hat. His lips canted in a half-smile.

"One of what, exactly?"

He shook his head and reached down to heft the trunk, almost effortlessly. "Where do you want this?"

"On my brother's carriage, but since he hasn't seemed to arrive…"

His eyes widened marginally. "You're Miss Chatham?"

"Mrs.," she corrected automatically, before she had the chance to be surprised that he knew her name. "And you are?"

He lifted his hat. "Judah Merrill. Sent by your brother to fetch you, it appears."

She straightened, and her pulse gave a little kick that she didn't want to analyze. "You're late," she said.

"The road to the ranch isn't quite as well-kept as the railway. Is this all you have?"

"There's more inside, as well as my maid."

He lifted his eyebrows. "More?" But without waiting for an answer, he turned and carted the trunk down to a buckboard wagon she hadn't noticed before.

"That is what my brother sent to fetch me?" she asked when the cowboy mounted the platform again.

"It's what we had available."

She looked at the rough conveyance in horror. It provided no padding, or shade, and looked ready to shake apart at the first bump.

"Your brother isn't a wealthy man, Mrs. Chatham. We have a working ranch and make do."

"You own the ranch as well?"

"I'm his foreman. The rest of your things are in there?" He nodded toward the depot.

After the wagon was loaded, he escorted her down the steps and handed her into the wagon. She arranged her skirts on the hard bench seat that would snag the fabric, as he assisted her maid into the back with the luggage. Then he swung into the seat beside her, the board on her end lifting with his added weight, and took up the reins.

She let her gaze drift to his hands. Long-fingered, strong, rough, so different from Neville's, or Nathan's. His sleeves were rolled back, something she didn't see men in San Francisco do. Men in society wore shirts and jackets buttoned up. But in this climate, that fashion would be impractical. And Mr. Merrill was a laborer, a man who worked for her brother. She forced her attention back to the conversation.

"How far is the ranch from here?"

"Couple of hours."

She cast a wary glance at the sun heading toward the hills. "Won't it be dark when we get there?"

"We'll be cutting it close." His tone was unconcerned. "That hat you brought won't do you much good against the sun here. Do you have a parasol?"

In San Francisco, she was more accustomed to hiding from the rain instead of the sun. She turned to retrieve the umbrella from Sonia, who also opened her own as she tried to get comfortable in the back of the wagon. At least her maid had the boards on the sides pinning her in. Rebecca feared one good bump would send her flying off this board and into the dirt.

"Is it always so hot here?" She was tempted to roll up her sleeves as Mr. Merrill had done.

A grin canted his lips. "This isn't nearly as hot as it's going to get." He slanted a look in her direction. "I've been to San Francisco, but it was in the winter. Doesn't it get hot there?"

"It's pleasantly warm now, but nothing like this. This steals your breath."

"You get used to it."

She lifted her skirts to allow the breeze to cool her ankles. She sincerely doubted she would be here long enough to get used to it. She would begin her campaign to come home as soon as she arrived at Gabriel's ranch. Her father had to forgive her.

"I enjoyed going to the ocean when I was there," Mr. Merrill continued. "Cold, but peaceful. I guess you'll miss that."

There were so many other things she'd miss, but that wasn't one of them. "I didn't go often."

"No? That's a shame. But I guess if you know it's there all the time, you tend to take things for granted."

Truer words had never been spoken, but she didn't want to linger on them. "What were you doing in San Francisco?"

"Ah. My older brother died. I went to claim his body."

"Oh." She pressed her hand to her chest. "My condolences."

"Thank you, but it's been a few years now."

"Is your family from there?"

He shook his head. "From Montana. My brother had come to start a saloon. The competition did not take kindly."

"He was killed?" A combination of horror and fascination washed over her. She had heard of such wild parts of the city, and Nathan had teased her about visiting, but she hadn't been quite so brave. She wondered if her young husband had gone there on his own, if that was where he had met his trouble.

"Yep."

"How horrible for you."

"Not my favorite experience."

The ride continued in silence, the back of the seat biting into her spine, her legs growing numb as the bare wood of the seat cut into the backs of her legs. A need began to make itself known. She looked about and saw nothing remotely resembling an outhouse, or any kind of cover, for that matter, not a tree or a bush in sight, only acres and acres of long, waving grass. She had no idea how long they'd been traveling, and was sure it wasn't more than a quarter of an hour, though the town was no longer in sight.

"Everything all right?" he asked when she shifted her weight.

"Certainly." How could she make her need known to this man, to this stranger? But she could hardly continue the rest of the journey in this fashion.

"Do you need to make a stop?"

"I—yes, but—" She stretched out her hand as if to ask where.

His shoulders relaxed, as if he was glad to have identified her problem. "I'll find you a spot. Probably would have been more comfortable for you back at the train depot."

She hadn't needed to go then, but didn't point that out. "I'm not accustomed to being so far from facilities," she retorted. "Please tell me my brother has indoor plumbing."

Mr. M made a sound of derision. "There's a privy not too far from the house, and a latrine for the bunkhouse."

Dismay heated her cheeks. A privy? How backwards was this place?

He continued on at a too-sedate pace for her peace of mind, before he finally pulled up, a few yards from a clump of trees. "Will that do?"

She braced her hand on the back of the wagon seat before he stopped her with a hand on her upper arm. She swung to face him.

"I'm going with you. There could be snakes."

She froze for a moment, but necessity had her scrambling down. "I'll be careful."

And she was, as careful as possible as she made her way to the far side of the trees and attended her needs. With a deep breath of relief—and a few curses for the number of petticoats that made the task nearly impossible—she moved away from the area and tried to figure out how to get back into her drawers without falling over.

She'd managed to get one leg in the garment when strange rustling sound drew her attention. A creature that almost blended in with the grass and dirt, as thick as her arm, coiled three feet away, its head drawn back, rattle hissing above the wind that blew through the grass. Startled, she dropped her skirts to run, just as it struck. Its fangs caught in the hem of her traveling suit, attached to her, so even if she ran, she wouldn't be safe. And if she shook it loose, it would strike again. The rattle became more insistent. Just as she decided to shake it loose and take her chances, the report of a gun echoed through the hills, and the snake split into two pieces, the head still stuck in her skirt, the body flopping, spraying blood.

She looked from the mangled mess to Mr. M, who lowered his rifle. That was the last thing she saw before she fell into a faint.

CHAPTER
Two

Judah caught her before she hit the ground, going down on his knees to do so. Good Lord, no wonder she fainted. The heat from her body almost seared him, and he felt the rigid corset beneath her blouse. When he bent to dislodge the snake head from the fabric of her skirt, he winced at the number of petticoats she wore. No woman in her right mind would be wearing so many clothes in this heat. He reached for the button of her skirt just as she stirred in his arms.

He turned his attention to her face as her eyes drifted open, lovely blue eyes that spit fire as soon as she took in what he was doing. She shoved at his chest and scrambled to her feet. She felt for her button, then, ensuring it was secure, she stepped back.

"You're too hot," he said. "You need to get rid of some of those petticoats."

She lifted her chin. "I'll arrive at my brother's house with all my clothes on, thank you."

"Though it may kill you?"

She looked unsure for a moment. "Turn your back."

He did, walking over to retrieve the body of the snake. Holy hell, it was a big one, four feet easy. "This'll make a fine belt."

"You can't be serious."

"Maybe a hat band, too." He touched the brim of his Stetson. "You doing all right over there? Shall I get your maid?"

"I'm...fine," she said amid little grunts of frustration and rustles of fabric. "Oh. Oh, dear."

He looked over his shoulder. Her face had gone white, and she was staring at a bloody bit of petticoat. He pivoted and bent to look at her ankle.

"Were you bitten?"

"No, it's the snake's blood. But goodness, there's a lot of it." A strange little giggle bubbled out of her throat.

He looked up and saw her eyes glaze over. He rose in a swift movement and gripped her arms. "You will not faint again, do you hear me? It's only a little blood."

He watched the struggle on her face as she lifted her gaze to his. "It's Parisian lace."

Something about the way she said it made him wonder if that was the real reason she'd gone so white, or if she was covering up her real fear. He grunted and released her. "Now your corset."

Her eyes widened. "No, I couldn't."

"I'll do it if you need to. Trust me when I saw Mrs. Lowell doesn't wear them."

She turned her head, and he thought she muttered something about Mrs. Lowell being a troglodyte.

"I can't have you fainting again. It's foolish to be wearing this many clothes in this heat."

"I'll be fine. The sun will be behind the hills soon."

Not soon enough, but he wouldn't waste any more time arguing with her. He scooped up the body of the snake from where he'd dropped it and started back to the wagon.

"You aren't really going to make a belt out of that, are you?" she asked, trotting along behind him, skirts lifted.

"Why not?"

She shuddered. "Because it's deadly."

He smirked and stretched the body out in his hands. It was a bit gruesome, so he covered the torn end with his hand. "Not anymore. Look at the patterns of his scales. Beautiful, aren't they?"

She looked, but didn't agree.

"Touch him. He's like nothing you've felt before."

She closed her delicate hand into a fist. "No, thank you."

He shrugged, walked to the back of the wagon, where he found an empty feed sack, dropped the body in, then hung it from the back of the wagon. He didn't want to frighten the poor maid. Stowing the rifle behind the wagon seat, he walked around to hand Mrs. Chatham into the wagon. She'd removed her gloves, and he wasn't wearing any, so when she placed her soft, slender hand in his...

Her gaze locked with his, and an unasked question furrowed her brow before she accepted his help into the wagon and picked up her parasol. He wished he knew what the hell that question was.

They didn't speak for a long stretch of time, which was fine by him, though he found himself wondering about her. She clearly didn't want to be here, didn't even seem to know much about the area, or the lifestyle, so why was she here? He was merely a hired hand and not privy to the gossip, but she was Mrs. Chatham, not Miss. Perhaps she was a recent widow, though she didn't wear black. Maybe she was destitute and had no choice. But Parisian lace, and the pride with which she determined to meet her brother...no, he couldn't figure her out.

———

He stopped at a stream to water the horses and to refill his canteen, which he offered to herself and then Sonia, before gulping. Rebecca couldn't help herself. She watched the play of muscles in his throat as he swallowed, the glint of sunlight on the dampness of his skin. When had she ever been attracted to a man who sweat? And yet Mr. Merrill—the way he handled the horses, the way he handled the rifle, blowing the snake into two in one shot—inches from her ankle—mercy. Perhaps the heat was taking its toll. She was being foolish.

But when he hefted himself back into the wagon beside her and those cinnamon-colored eyes flashed at her, she was lost.

She didn't know how long after the stream they paused again. She saw nothing around and so looked at him curiously.

"This is the beginning of your brother's land."

"With no fences? How do you know?"

"He has a few closer to the house."

"Are we close now? How much land does he have?"

"A couple hundred acres, a couple hundred head of cattle, and about twenty horses."

"I thought you said he wasn't wealthy. That sounds wealthy to me. So many horses."

"We're breeding them, hoping to get some good trotting pairs, carriage horses. If he can get a reputation there, he can be a rich man. In the meantime, he raises cattle to cover expenses."

"Which part of the operation do you oversee?"

He grinned. "I have my hands in all of it."

Her heart sank as they crested a rise and she saw the house for the first time. It was long and low, whitewashed, crude. At least it was on a hill and not down in one of the stifling valleys. The house was surrounded by a wooden porch and mismatched chairs were set out on it, perhaps so people could catch a breeze. Clothes fluttered on the line, odd for so late in the day, but what did Rebecca know about housekeeping and laundry? Other items cluttered the yard, an overturned wash bucket, miscellaneous farming gear and...a perfectly good carriage. Rebecca snapped her gaze to Mr. Merrill, who shrugged. "It's unsuitable for the roads we just traveled, but they do use it for church."

More likely, they didn't use it for her because they wanted to send her a message. She wasn't welcome here. Rebecca wanted to cry as she recalled the lovely three-story house she'd left behind.

Beyond the house was another long building. The bunkhouse, perhaps. And beyond that, the stables and a barn. A decent spread, she supposed, but what was she supposed to do here? Laundry?

Just then a man came out of the house, and Rebecca jolted. Gabriel looked and moved just like their father, though their father would never be caught in such rough clothing. Behind him, Beatrice appeared in the doorway, heavier than she'd been the last time Rebecca had seen her. Of course, she had three little ones now, and Rebecca had seen more than one woman spread after a pregnancy.

Neither of them smiled, but then, this wasn't exactly a welcome visit, was it? Rebecca squared her shoulders, wishing she'd put her jacket back on, another layer of armor, wishing her hair wasn't falling down, wishing...

No use of that, now, was there? She folded her hands in her lap and looked down her nose at her brother as he approached to help her out of the wagon. He took her hand, and gave her a pointed look at her lack of gloves. She rose with a toss of her head and a swish of her skirts, and hopped from the wagon with as little help from him as possible. She stumbled a bit, then snapped her spine straight and looked past Gabriel to Beatrice's pinched face.

"Sister. I trust you had a safe journey."

She decided to forego the snake incident and merely nodded. "And quite long. I would love a bath and bed."

"We saved supper for you," Beatrice said, sounding affronted.

"That sounds lovely as well." Did that mean she had to sit with them at the table? The food would curdle in her stomach if they continued looking at her in such a way.

She managed to put one foot in front of the other as she heard Mr. Merrill unloading her luggage.

"So much!" Beatrice exclaimed. "Where will we put it all?"

"It can go in the barn," Gabriel said. "You don't need that much out here."

The barn! With rats and mice? Her wardrobe cost a fortune. The delicate fabrics needed special care. She wanted to argue but

CHAPTER
Three

"Do you need a hand?" Judah asked, though he doubted he could approach her without revealing how the sight of her in her transparent chemise affected him.

"I can manage."

But she winced as she closed her fingers around the rope. He thought of those delicate hands on the rough rope, thought of how exhausted she'd been when they arrived, and he willed his body to behave as he walked up the rise to take the rope from her hand. He expected her to cover her nakedness, or run back into the house, but she did neither, and that raised his interest. Why not? Pride, he suspected, but more than that. Nonetheless, he kept his gaze averted despite every temptation, and lifted the bucket in only a few pulls. A glance at her hands told her she'd gotten a splinter or two, maybe some blisters. Hard to tell with just the moonlight.

Maybe that explained her modesty. Maybe she thought he couldn't see her nipples and the triangle of hair between her legs because it was dark. Little did she know that chemise was like a beacon of light, and if she wasn't careful, would draw the interest of a man besides himself.

He emptied the bucket into the basin. "Do you need more?"

"No, this will do. Thank you."

"Shall I carry it to your room for you?"

Her gaze flicked to his, and behind the wariness he saw something else—curiosity, maybe?

"Thank you, no. I'm sharing a room with Sonia and she'll be waiting for her own bath."

"Not as adventurous as you?" He couldn't keep his gaze from lowering to her erect nipples. God help him. His mouth dried at the thought of sipping the sweet flesh into his mouth.

"I'm only adventurous when the situation calls for it."

But he could have sworn a blush colored her cheeks and chest. She hefted the basin in both arms, dangling the pitcher beneath, and some of the water sloshed over the sides.

"Whoa, there. Let me get it. You're barely on your feet." He slipped his arms beneath hers, his elbow brushing her breast, and lifted the basin. "You get the door."

For a moment, she looked like she wanted to argue, but then she nodded and walked ahead of him in that sheer damp chemise that showed the cleft of her heart-shaped ass. He heaved out a long breath, as if that would help, before he followed her. She swung the door open, then marched across the hall and opened another door, where Sonia cowed on her bed at his sudden appearance. Her eyes widened when she looked past him to her disheveled mistress, but she remained silent.

"Just there will do," Mrs. Chatham said, pointing to a table.

He set the basin down, then turned back to her, longing to lift that heavy hair in his hands to feel it, longing to strip that wet fabric from her body and taste her skin. He hadn't been with a woman in so long, and his body was reminding him, very insistently.

The boss's sister. Bad, bad idea. As if she would even look twice at him, a city woman and a cowboy.

"The creek we crossed aways back? It winds around and runs behind the house here. Might be better for bathing than the middle of the yard."

She nodded shortly, and he tipped his hat, then slipped outside, in search of that same creek, where he could cool off and forget about Mrs. Chatham.

―――――

Rebecca was roused early from sleep by her sister-in-law's presence in her bedroom.

"Time to get up, Mrs. Lazy Bones," Beatrice ordered. "There's work that needs to be done. This won't be a free ride for you the way it was at home."

Rebecca blinked up at Beatrice and wanted to slap the sneer off the other woman's face. No doubt she knew the reason Rebecca had been sent here, probably knew more about her exile than Rebecca did. And she had no doubt Beatrice had trouble in store for her. She sat up and allowed the rough sheet of her bed to fall to her waist, revealing her nakedness. Beatrice blanched, then colored and backed up, her lips pressed together.

"Get dressed and come to the kitchen if you want to eat. Then I have chores for you."

Chores. Rebecca hadn't had chores since, well, ever. She'd been told to straighten her room as a girl. Sometimes she did, sometimes she didn't. She'd been told to care for her horse after a ride in the park, but usually she could charm one of the grooms to do it for her. She wondered what hell Beatrice had in store for her.

―――――

This, she had not expected. Rebecca did her best to corral her oldest nephew David, while balancing her niece Betsy—a playful name for her solemn brother and his wife to call their only daughter—on her hip. Her middle nephew Vernon took advantage of her distraction and bolted down the hill to the stable. Rebecca snatched David's hand and took off after Vernon. The last thing she needed was for the child to get into the stable and cause mischief.

Suddenly, the child slowed, and she did too, when she saw what he saw.

There in the center of the corral outside the stable, stood Mr. Merrill, wearing what looked to be a thermal undershirt tucked into his jeans, his hat tilted back just a bit as he followed the movement of a horse at the end of a long line. His concentration was absolute on the roan gelding, his posture complete calm. She thought she heard him murmur something to the horse, who picked up his pace from a trot to a canter. Still, Mr. Merrill followed him easily. Then with another murmur, the horse dropped back to a trot, then a walk. The animal tossed his head, but kept a steady pace at Mr. Merrill's urging.

Then Mr. Merrill saw her.

She gathered up the children and walked to the edge of the corral. "He's a lovely animal. Do you ride him?"

"I'm working on training him with voice commands so he can be a carriage horse. But yes, I ride him occasionally." He turned his attention to the young ones, still for the first time since Beatrice shoved them at her this morning. "I see you have your new duty."

Betsy wriggled in her arms, but Rebecca refused to put her down. "Perhaps I can borrow some of your halters to keep them all in one place."

He laughed, and the low, husky sound struck a chord deep inside her. "Maybe we could arrange that." He grinned down at David. "What do you say, little bronc? Want a halter like Rojo, here?"

The boy broke free from Rebecca and climbed up on the split-rail fence to come face to face with Mr. Merrill. "Yes!"

Mr. Merrill laughed again and climbed the fence in two moves, picking up David and placing him on the ground in front of Rebecca. "Not used to being around little ones?"

She shook her head. "I don't think my sister-in-law could have found a more unsuitable chore."

"You and Mr. Chatham don't have children?"

She thought of her young, handsome husband, the wild house parties, the amazing lovemaking, the joy, the frivolity, the heartbreak. "No room for children," she murmured. "That was always going to be in the future, until there was no more future."

"He passed?"

"In a manner of speaking."

Little Vernon wiggled free from her grasp, and she went running again.

"I have those halters in the barn," he called after her, and she was very very tempted.

If Rebecca had thought that her trip had been exhausting, it was nothing to taking care of three children, none of whom ever stopped. She thought children napped, but clearly that was a lie. They'd finally gone to bed shortly after dinner. Physically drained, Rebecca still hadn't wanted to go into that tiny room she shared with Sonia—and poor Sonia. If Rebecca had been put to work, she didn't want to know what poor Sonia had done all day.

She walked outside after an unpleasant dinner with silent Gabriel and smug Beatrice. She considered going down to the stables in search of Mr. Merrill. He'd been at the edge of her thoughts all day, the easy way he'd been with the children, his laugh, the way he'd looked as he guided the horse. The play of his muscles intrigued her. She'd never enjoyed watching a man work, never enjoyed watching sweat trickle down a man's face, never enjoyed seeing the satisfaction on a man's face as he completed a task.

Okay, perhaps she had done all those things, but not while a man was clothed. Which brought her to the image of Mr. Merrill unclothed. He would be lean and muscular, and the hint of chest hair she'd seen peeking from the opening of his shirt would add a lovely texture as her breasts rubbed against him.

Mmm. She lifted a hand to rub the back of her neck, as if that could cool her thoughts. Wouldn't it make Beatrice crazy if Rebecca had an affair with the ranch foreman?

A light in the stables drew her, and she made her way down the hill, heart pounding. She had been bold in the past, but always she was certain of a man's reaction. With Mr. Merrill, she couldn't be sure. But he was the only person nice to her, and she didn't want to go to her room yet.

As she expected, he was in the stable, his back to her, rubbing down Rojo's coat with a currycomb. She listened to the soothing sound of his voice as he spoke to the horse, but before she could make herself known, the horse turned his head in her direction, and so did Mr. Merrill. Surprise lifted his eyebrows for a moment, but she didn't let that stop her. She continued forward and stopped on the other side of Rojo's head.

"Come looking for those harnesses?" he asked.

She blew out an unladylike snort that startled the horse, but Mr. Merrill soothed him with soft sounds. "Beatrice had the nerve to tell me I needed to stay in the house in case one of the children woke up. I told her I believed they were her children and she could see to them for the night."

"I'm sure she took that well."

She gave in to the urge to stroke her hand down Rojo's big neck. "I don't want to be in the house right now. Are you taking him out?" She noticed the saddle draped over the nearby stall door.

"Yeah, we like our evening rides."

The idea was so appealing, galloping under the moonlight in the blessedly cool evening, the wind blowing, the freedom—how she missed her freedom.

"Would you like to go?"

Her heart tripped at the invitation. "I can't ride in this," she said mournfully, lifting her skirt.

He frowned, looking at the garment, then moved to saddle the horse. "You don't have a riding habit in all those clothes you brought?"

"It's in the house, and I'd prefer not to go back there just yet."

He grunted and cinched the saddle around Rojo's belly. The horse shifted, as if anxious to be on his way. Mr. Merrill slipped the bridle on with a fluid movement and led the horse from the stall. Again he inspected her skirt.

"I don't have a sidesaddle, but I have a thought."

Before she could ask what it was, he closed his hands around her waist and lifted her sideways onto the saddle.

"Hook your knee over the saddle horn," he said. When he was satisfied she'd done as he told her, he swung up behind her, looping a hand around her waist and drawing her back against his hard chest. "Good?"

Breathless with the suddenness of his decision, and with the intimacy of his arm around her, she could only nod. The muscles of his thighs moved against her bottom as he urged Rojo forward, out of the barn, then to a trot as they headed down the road, then to a canter over the field. Even in her precarious position, she felt secure in Mr. Merrill's strong embrace. Her hair came loose from its pins and she laughed as he shoved it out of his face, lowering them both over Rojo's back and urging the big horse faster.

Finally they pulled up beside the creek they had crossed yesterday. Mr. Merrill swung off, then lifted his arms to her. She placed her hands on his upper arms and felt them flex as he carried her down. Goodness. She'd never known a man to be so hard all over, and she didn't release him right away. Her heart fluttered when she realized he hadn't released her, either.

"You took my advice about the corset," he said.

She should be appalled. Gentlemen didn't speak to ladies about their undergarments, no matter the context. Instead she swayed just a little closer, enjoying the heat of his hands on her skin through the thin cotton of her shirtwaist. Her skirts swirled around the horse's legs, spooking him just a bit, and Mr. Merrill released her to calm the animal.

She walked toward the stream and sat on a boulder. "The way you ride him, one would think you have no fear."

"I have plenty. But he and I understand each other." He rubbed the horse's muzzle before dropping the reins to the ground.

"He'll stay without being tethered?" She had a sudden fear of the horse taking off, leaving her and Mr. Merrill to walk back in the dead of night. How far had they ridden? It had felt like no time, but when they'd arrived yesterday, the distance from the creek to the house had seemed to take forever.

"He'll stay." He walked to the boulder where she sat.

"Do you ride every night?"

"If I can. Sometimes I have to stay close, but this is my time."

"And I'm intruding on it."

He tucked her hair behind her ear. "I wouldn't have brought you along if I didn't want to."

She tilted her head to feel his fingers against her skin, and he dropped his hand away as if she'd burned him. She held back a sigh. Of course he was honorable and wouldn't act on her invitations unless she was very clear. She wasn't sure she was ready to be very clear just yet.

"Tell me about the horses."

He settled on the boulder a respectable distance from her. "What do you want to know about the horses?"

"Do you buy them? Raise them? And then train them?"

"A combination of the two. Raising them takes a bit longer on the investment. Why? You looking to get out of nanny duty?" His teeth flashed white in the moonlight.

She laughed again. "Do you think Beatrice would let me?"

"Why are you here?"

The abruptness of his question stilled her laugh. "What?"

"It seems clear you didn't come here to care for your brother's children. And you aren't accustomed to life outside of a city. So why?"

Her face heated, and she considered telling him it was none of his business. She didn't want him to think poorly of her. That itself surprised her, because when was the last time she cared what someone thought of her?

"There was a scandal and my family preferred me out of the city."

"A scandal?" A laugh colored his question. "Let me guess. You rode out with a man you barely know without a chaperone."

She wrinkled her nose. "They certainly wouldn't approve of that, either. But no."

"What did you do that had your family send you out here?"

His curiosity surprised her, but she supposed she was a target for it. But she couldn't bring herself to tell him another man had been kissing her breasts. She wasn't a whore, despite what people thought. She was only lonely. And she enjoyed the attention of men. If Mr. Merrill knew the scandal that had brought her here, he would treat her just as Beatrice and her brother did.

Instead of answering, she tilted her head to look at the endless stretch of stars. She never paid attention to the stars in the city, wasn't even sure she would be able to see them. "Do you ever sleep out here?"

He was quiet a moment as he processed the fact that she wouldn't share her secret. "Sometimes. I didn't bring my gear this time, though."

"I imagine it's cooler here than a bunkhouse."

"Less crowded, too."

She understood that. She'd been devastated over giving up the house she had shared with Nathan, where she'd had freedom, and moving back to the room from her childhood. But even that room had been enormous when compared to the room she now shared with her maid.

She leaned her head back, letting the breeze caress her throat. "Have you been married?"

Silence dragged before he asked, "Why do you ask that?"

"You seem to be comfortable with women in a way unmarried men aren't."

Another silence. "I was. She died."

"In Montana?"

"You remember that?"

She looked sideways at him. "You told me yesterday."

He chuckled. "True. Yes. In Montana."

"Any children?"

"No. We weren't married long."

His suddenly brisk tone, at odds with his usual laconic drawl, told her he didn't want to pursue the topic. Of course that only raised more questions in her head. Had he been madly in love with his wife? How long had they been married? How did she die? But she wouldn't ask, since she wouldn't answer for him.

She smoothed her fingers over the boulder beside her thoughtfully. "We were married three years. I wonder if having children would have changed things."

"Changed what things?"

"We were…very imprudent. Perhaps having children would have given us a better sense of responsibility. Perhaps I'd be as upstanding as my brother Gabriel."

"Having children doesn't always make people responsible," he said in a way that made her think he knew more about it than he wanted to share.

"Perhaps. And as you saw, I'm not precisely the maternal type."

He chuckled again. "Maybe you should start small. The barn cat has kittens."

"I'm sure I could corral them no better than my brother's children. Are they always so wild?"

"I imagine they're taking advantage of your inexperience. You'll find a way."

In the distance, she heard a howl and edged closer to him. She hadn't thought of the predators that might be out at this time of night. "Wolf?" she asked.

"Coyote. He won't come close."

The lone howl was followed by several yips and responding howls, and to Rebecca, it seemed they were surrounded. Rojo lifted his head and snorted his dislike of the noise.

"Did you bring your rifle?" She hadn't noticed it when he was saddling Rojo.

"I have my six-shooter." He gestured to the gun at his hip.

"That sounded like more than six animals."

"If they come close, shooting one will scare them off." He eased his hand behind her back. "I took you for having more guts than that."

"I fear I may have misled you," she said with a nervous laugh, straining to see in the darkness, but feeling slightly safer with his arm nearby. She couldn't say why.

"Do you want to go back?"

She looked up at him. "You don't think we are in danger?"

He shook his head. "Coyotes are cowards, and usually pick on a young calf or sheep. We're too big for them. Now mountain lions…"

A jolt went through her. "Mountain lions! You're not saying there are mountain lions around here?"

"On occasion. Don't go far from the house without someone with a gun."

"Perhaps I should learn to shoot."

He took a breath and held it a moment as he considered. "Tomorrow. Once you get out of nanny duty, I'll take you out away from the house and show you how to fire a gun."

The idea of spending more time with him, one on one, sent a thrill through her. Would he put his arms around her, touch her to arrange her stance? Did he want to touch her?

"That is, if your brother says it's all right."

"Do you think he would say no?"

Mr. Merrill lifted his hat, then settled it farther back on his head. "He has very definite ideas about what a lady should and shouldn't do."

She adjusted her skirts to provide more padding against the boulder. "It's unlikely he would approve of me riding out here with you tonight."

"Very unlikely."

"And yet you didn't hesitate to bring me along," she pressed, wanting him to give her some clue as to his intent.

"I got the feeling you needed to get away."

Ah. So he felt sorry for her. She stretched back with a sigh. "And it's only been one day." Relaxation loosened her muscles as she watched the stars. She had no idea how long they sat there in silence, but suddenly she was opening her eyes.

"I'd better get you back," Mr. Merrill said.

"Was I asleep?" she asked, rolling her head on her neck. Her cheek was numb, and when she rubbed it, she realized she'd had her head on his shoulder.

"I believe that's what the snoring meant."

"I do not snore," she protested.

He stroked a hand down her back. "You do."

She warmed at the intimate caress, at the knowledge he'd allowed her to rest against him. "How long?"

"Long enough that I'd better get you back." He stood and took her hand to help her to her feet, steadying her when she swayed.

She let herself lean against his chest for a moment, warm and firm, and the next thing she knew, he was lifting her into the saddle. "A girl could get used to all this being carried around."

"A man could get used to having his arms around a beautiful woman," he replied, swinging into the saddle behind her and pulling her closer than he'd held her on the ride out.

His scent surrounded her, warm and male and earthy. Oh, how she missed being held by a man, feeling the differences in their bodies. She loved everything about a man's body, the strength, the roughness, the hardness. She loved everything about sex. Almost without thinking, she shifted her hip to rest more

He frowned, looking at the garment, then moved to saddle the horse. "You don't have a riding habit in all those clothes you brought?"

"It's in the house, and I'd prefer not to go back there just yet."

He grunted and cinched the saddle around Rojo's belly. The horse shifted, as if anxious to be on his way. Mr. Merrill slipped the bridle on with a fluid movement and led the horse from the stall. Again he inspected her skirt.

"I don't have a sidesaddle, but I have a thought."

Before she could ask what it was, he closed his hands around her waist and lifted her sideways onto the saddle.

"Hook your knee over the saddle horn," he said. When he was satisfied she'd done as he told her, he swung up behind her, looping a hand around her waist and drawing her back against his hard chest. "Good?"

Breathless with the suddenness of his decision, and with the intimacy of his arm around her, she could only nod. The muscles of his thighs moved against her bottom as he urged Rojo forward, out of the barn, then to a trot as they headed down the road, then to a canter over the field. Even in her precarious position, she felt secure in Mr. Merrill's strong embrace. Her hair came loose from its pins and she laughed as he shoved it out of his face, lowering them both over Rojo's back and urging the big horse faster.

Finally they pulled up beside the creek they had crossed yesterday. Mr. Merrill swung off, then lifted his arms to her. She placed her hands on his upper arms and felt them flex as he carried her down. Goodness. She'd never known a man to be so hard all over, and she didn't release him right away. Her heart fluttered when she realized he hadn't released her, either.

"You took my advice about the corset," he said.

She should be appalled. Gentlemen didn't speak to ladies about their undergarments, no matter the context. Instead she swayed just a little closer, enjoying the heat of his hands on her skin through the thin cotton of her shirtwaist. Her skirts swirled around the horse's legs, spooking him just a bit, and Mr. Merrill released her to calm the animal.

She walked toward the stream and sat on a boulder. "The way you ride him, one would think you have no fear."

"I have plenty. But he and I understand each other." He rubbed the horse's muzzle before dropping the reins to the ground.

"He'll stay without being tethered?" She had a sudden fear of the horse taking off, leaving her and Mr. Merrill to walk back in the dead of night. How far had they ridden? It had felt like no time, but when they'd arrived yesterday, the distance from the creek to the house had seemed to take forever.

"He'll stay." He walked to the boulder where she sat.

"Do you ride every night?"

"If I can. Sometimes I have to stay close, but this is my time."

"And I'm intruding on it."

He tucked her hair behind her ear. "I wouldn't have brought you along if I didn't want to."

She tilted her head to feel his fingers against her skin, and he dropped his hand away as if she'd burned him. She held back a sigh. Of course he was honorable and wouldn't act on her invitations unless she was very clear. She wasn't sure she was ready to be very clear just yet.

"Tell me about the horses."

He settled on the boulder a respectable distance from her. "What do you want to know about the horses?"

"Do you buy them? Raise them? And then train them?"

"A combination of the two. Raising them takes a bit longer on the investment. Why? You looking to get out of nanny duty?" His teeth flashed white in the moonlight.

She laughed again. "Do you think Beatrice would let me?"

"Why are you here?"

The abruptness of his question stilled her laugh. "What?"

"It seems clear you didn't come here to care for your brother's fully against his groin, and thought she could feel him responding to her, even through her petticoats. She didn't move away, only focused on the sensations of his arms around her. He walked the horse back, and each step was like the rhythm of sex, slow and deliberate, his hips rolling against hers, his sex hard with each stroke. But he didn't move away, and neither did she.

She was nearly boneless with longing as he stopped Rojo outside the stall and swung from the saddle, then brought her down. This time, Rojo's restlessness didn't distract him. He slid her the length of his body so her skirts snagged between them. His fingers closed around her waist and he held her for a moment, until she looked up at him. He didn't smile, exactly, but something glinted in his cinnamon-colored eyes before he bent his head and brushed his lips over hers. Just that one simple caress sent heat racing through her body, her pulse pounding in places too long neglected. She whispered, "Yes," against his mouth and wound her arms around his broad shoulders, pressing her breasts against his chest.

He made a sound deep in his throat, pulled her closer and covered her mouth with his, a claiming kiss that made her skin tingle. His stubble rasped her skin. He tasted nice, minty, unexpected, as he tilted his head and slipped his tongue between her lips. She curled her fingers in the thick hair at the back of his neck, holding him to her as his tongue explored, as she lifted hers to meet his and return the intimate caress.

He shuffled his feet a bit, and she found her back pressed against the wall of the stall, his hands tight on her waist, his knee between hers, tangling in her skirts, holding his hips just out of reach of where she wanted to feel him, hip to hip, wanted to feel his sex against her, right at the core of her. They would measure up just right, if only he would lean closer. Why didn't he touch her? She wanted him to touch her everywhere, wanted to feel his rough fingertips against her skin, wanted to feel his hands on her breasts. Just the thought made her sex grow damp.

Her restless fingers wound into the fabric of his shirt at his shoulders, when she wanted nothing more than to work his buttons open and slide over his chest, where the hint of hair teased her. Her husband had been smooth-chested, but she wanted to feel the roughness of hair against her breasts. What would he do if she loosened his buttons and slid her hands inside?

Suddenly, he broke the kiss, his expression dazed as he looked down at her.

"I'm sorry, Mrs. Chatham. I shouldn't have done that."

"Mrs. Chatham?" His formality amused her. She touched her fingers to her lips, her gaze on his mouth. His lips had been surprisingly soft amidst the prickly facial hair. So many sensations to absorb—she had missed some. Would he indulge her in an encore performance? She forced her gaze to his. He was apologizing, after all. "I'm Rebecca."

His cheeks were red. "I shouldn't have taken liberties."

"I invited them, Judah."

He drew a breath through his nose at her use of his given name. "You know what I mean. I'm a working man. You're a lady."

Not anymore. She turned her hand from her lips to his. "Say my name, Judah."

His eyes flicked to her mouth. "Rebecca."

She smiled. "May I come riding with you again tomorrow?"

"Your brother—"

"Has no business knowing." Once she was certain he wouldn't be kissing her any more tonight, she stepped sideways, away from the wall. "Thank you, Judah. Good night."

Rebecca lay on her back and stared at the ceiling in the windowless room, listening to the even breathing of Sonia in the other cot, but unable to sleep herself as she relived every touch, every kiss. Her lips still burned from the prickle of his stubble, her hips likely bore the imprint of his fingers. She wondered what would have happened if he hadn't had an attack of conscience. She wouldn't have stopped him, as aroused as she was. Would he have made love to her against the wall, or in the hay? Dangerous, both places, with the chance of discovery. Did he know how to please a woman? Did he know about the clitoris, and cunnilingus and fellatio? She wouldn't mind helping him discover the last, going down on her knees before him, and taking his length into her mouth, giving him pleasure with her lips and tongue. Imagining his expression made her sex ache, and she pressed her hand to it through her shift.

She had loved sex with her husband, and he'd shown her so much. Theirs had been a grand passion, and they'd created scandal wherever they went because they couldn't keep their hands off each other. They'd dallied in gardens, had sex in carriages—her favorite. They'd been caught in alcoves and once, when the lights were down in the theater, she'd stroked him to orgasm in the midst of the audience. He'd returned the favor in the ladies' powder room.

She missed the contact, missed the pleasure her own touch couldn't give her. But Judah's could. She determined to help him overcome his own conscience.

In the meantime, she quietly stroked herself to release, imagining Judah's mouth in place of her fingers.

Rebecca was at her wits' end the next morning. Her niece and nephews had been screaming from the time they woke up this morning. Beatrice merely sat at the table with her own breakfast, leaving the three children without. She flicked a gaze at Rebecca. Anger stiffened her shoulders as she went to the stove to serve the children.

But she understood. Beatrice didn't want her here, and Rebecca would be punished for her presence.

She took the little ones outside, because she needed to be away from her sister-in-law, but the children didn't want to be contained within the yard. Rebecca was too proud to ask Beatrice how she had kept the children occupied before her arrival.

"I'll make a bargain with you." Exhausted from chasing the children around the small area, Rebecca was desperate. "If you eat all your lunch and lay down for one hour, I will take you to play with kittens." And she had the added bonus of possibly encountering Judah.

"Kittens!" Betsy squealed, and the three of them marched into the kitchen in a perfect imitation of well-behaved children.

The afternoon was spent in the warm hay of the stable, with kittens crawling from one lap to another before collapsing in exhaustion. Giggles echoed off the rafters as the mother cat watched the activity, laying on her side and extending her paws in rhythmic stretches. Just like Beatrice, wanting someone else to take care of her children.

Judah was nowhere in sight. Perhaps he'd forgotten his promise to teach her to shoot. Likely he had other chores that took him out on the land with the cattle. Rojo was missing, she saw. She tried not to look for him like a lovesick girl.

Betsy needed to use the privy, so Rebecca herded them to the one close to the house.

Just then, Judah rode up on Rojo. He swung down beside her and picked a piece of hay from her hair.

"What have you been doing?"

She angled her head and shifted toward him, so her skirts swayed over his boots. "Playing with the kittens. Their reward for eating their lunch and taking a nap."

He looked from her to the children. "And where are you heading now?"

"The privy."

Finally he moved back, just a half-step. "Think you can break away for shooting lessons?"

She shook her head. "I don't think Beatrice will allow it. After dinner, perhaps?"

He nodded, touched his hat, and led Rojo away.

———

Rebecca said nothing after dinner, just slipped out as soon as she cleared her plate and headed down to the barn. Her heart thundered with anticipation at being alone with him. Her skin prickled with the thought that he might kiss her again. If he didn't, she would kiss him. Perhaps this time she could get him to touch her as well.

Judah was sitting in the tack room, polishing a harness. He looked up and gave her that slow smile that sent heat sliding through her body and pooling between her legs.

"Beatrice let you go?"

"Not exactly. Perhaps we should head off before she comes looking for me."

He rose slowly and started out of the barn.

"Aren't we going to take Rojo?"

"The guns spook him, so we're going to walk a little ways, over the rise there." He pointed.

"I'm to shoot your revolver?" She gestured to the weapon at his hip.

"For starters. The rifle has a bit of a kick. I want to see how you do with this today. We can do the rifle another day."

"Providing I'm allowed to leave the house again."

He smiled. "Just tell your brother you're learning to shoot to protect the children."

"Those children need very little protection. I believe they're tougher and faster than anything we might see out here."

He laughed. "They are busy. Good thinking, bringing them to the barn to see the cats."

"Tomorrow I'm going to bribe them with going to the stream to play. Then I need to come up with some more activities."

"When I was a boy, my mother had a schedule for us. And we had chores. I'd say the boys are old enough for chores already."

They walked over the rise until they were out of sight of the house.

"Wait here." Judah strode forward in measured steps, then stooped and gathered twigs into a pyramid shape, then rose and walked back to her, drawing his revolver from his holster and standing in front of her, feet apart, gun extended in both hands. "That'll do as your target for now. All right. Always treat a gun as if it is loaded, and keep it pointed where it will do the least amount of harm. Never ever point it at a person unless you mean to kill him. I keep it pointed down, and I keep it on an empty chamber so it doesn't accidentally go off and kill someone." He popped the cylinder out and showed her the five bullets and one empty chamber. Then he closed it with a snick and held it in both hands for her to inspect. "Barrel, sight, cylinder, trigger guard, trigger, hammer, grip. Got it?"

She nodded.

"Tell me."

She recited and pointed. She had always been a quick study.

"Okay, take it by the grip and point the barrel at the ground."

She closed her hand over the wooden grip, warm from being worn against his body, and lifted it from his hands. "It's heavier than I thought."

"Yep. You'll get used to it. Maybe not today." He stepped beside her and turned to face the makeshift target. "You'll need to use both hands to raise it."

She did, and felt the weight of the weapon in her upper arms and shoulders. She lowered the barrel a fraction of an inch, and he angled it up, then moved his hands to her elbows to straighten her arms.

"How's that feel?"

"I can't hold it for long."

"Sure you can. Now, part your feet just a bit, so they're even with your shoulders. This will give you some stability."

She wriggled her feet apart. He was standing so close she was having trouble concentrating. Each word floated over her skin, bringing back the memory of his kiss, his mouth on her. She wanted to feel his mouth all over. Perhaps, after her lesson, she could tempt him into complying.

"All right. Now the sight," he said, oblivious to her line of thought. "See that little piece of metal sticking up there? That's what you want to point at the target. You look at the sight, but the target beyond looks blurry. You understand what I'm saying?"

"It looks blurry," she said obediently.

"Good. Now. Ease back the hammer with your thumb. You remember which is the hammer?"

She tapped the device.

"Good girl. Now slowly draw it back."

The muscles of her thumb ached as she drew back the hammer.

"Not far enough. That's half-cocked. You want it full-cocked. Pull it a little more."

She did, feeling the strain, but he relaxed as she completed the task.

"Check your sight again. Are you aimed at the target?"

She nodded.

"All right. You're going to put your finger on the trigger and press on it until it fires. It's going to be loud, and it's going to startle you. Just be aware."

She nodded, took a deep breath, and pressed, feeling the strain in the palm of her hand. And then it clicked silently, the hammer dropping back into place.

"All right. That was the empty chamber. Do it again."

Squaring her shoulders, she drew the hammer back to half-cock, then full cock, replaced her finger on the trigger and repeated. The gun kicked up in her hands as it fired, the report echoing off the hills. Judah steadied her with his hands on her shoulders, chuckling a bit. When she regained her balance, she peered at the target to see it hadn't been touched. She scowled.

"I want to try it again."

"Good. Let's try something else." He moved behind her, adjusting her shoulders, then sliding his hands down her arms to her elbows, supporting them.

Her nipples hardened at the proximity of his hands. "I can't think when you do that."

He chuckled, his breath stirring her hair. "Sure you can. I'm just going to keep you from falling back when the gun fires. Check the sight. Are you aimed at the target?"

She adjusted, then nodded.

"Okay, then. Shoot."

She pressed the trigger and winced at the report. When she opened her eyes, she saw grass kick up to the left of the target.

"Better," he said, too close to her ear.

Suddenly, she didn't want to shoot anymore, just wanted to turn in his arms and kiss him, but she wasn't a quitter. Besides, the way he put his hands on her was like a seduction, like a dance under the darkening sky.

"Again," she said, a bit breathless.

"That's my girl."

Pride strengthening her at his praise, she fired again and again until the cylinder was empty, still not hitting the target. She sighed in frustration and lowered the gun as he drew fresh bullets from his pocket.

"Now open the cylinder. I'll show you how to load it." He demonstrated by placing the first bullet in place, then allowed her to fill the rest of the cylinder.

Her fingers shook, but she wasn't sure if it was desire at his nearness or desire to please him. The soothing sound of his deep voice rolled over her. She'd never known a man so patient, so willing to let her move at her own pace, and she wondered if he would be like that as they made love. She dropped a bullet at that thought of his hands stroking her slowly, of his body moving over hers with the same deliberateness.

He held onto her waist as he bent to collect the bullet from the grass, and he held it out to her with a crooked smile that made her wonder if he knew what she was thinking. She plucked the bullet from his fingers and placed it into the cylinder, pushing the thoughts of making love to him aside.

Once the gun was loaded, she stepped away from him, wanting to try it on her own, and fired. The pyramid of grass exploded as the bullet plowed through it and she turned, delighted, and flung her arms about his neck. He reached behind him to reclaim the gun, then returned her embrace, drawing her closer. She eased back to look up at him, torn between remaining in his arms and repeating her success. She slid her palm down his arm and closed her fingers around his gun hand.

"I want to do it again."

He laughed, a sound that vibrated against her breasts, and relinquished the gun as she backed away, her gaze holding his. She turned and emptied the revolver, hitting the pyramid twice more. When she lowered the gun, arms tingling, shoulders aching, she turned to him, unable to hide the smile of pride. He took the gun from her, holstered it, then took her face in his hands and kissed her.

Yes. This. She closed her hands around his, stroking their lean strength, and leaned into him, teasing his lips with the tip of her tongue. He drew in a quick breath and curved his hand around the back of her head, angling her as he took the kiss deeper, his lips parting hers, his tongue sliding inside her mouth to taste her. The roughness of his evening beard pricked her lips, but she rose on her toes and pressed closer, savoring the differences between them. She swayed forward until he slid his hands to her hips, drawing her against him, breasts to chest, hip to hip, his arousal apparent even through her heavy skirt. Instinctively, she parted her feet and moved against it, until he growled low in his throat. Before he could protest, she took his hand from her hip and guided it to her aching breast, desire flooding her as he rubbed her nipple with his thumb. She didn't want to break contact with him, but the urge to touch his chest was too great. She slipped her hands between them and opened the top button of his shirt.

He captured her wrist and broke the kiss. "We'll get Rojo and go for a ride."

She blinked up at him, then nodded. He took her hand and headed back over the rise.

Rebecca briefly considered running to the house to change into her riding habit, as she'd planned earlier, but didn't want to be cornered by Beatrice. Instead, she followed Judah into the barn, her entire body craving his touch, his weight over her, his heavy arousal sliding into her. If he brought a bedroll, they could make love under the stars.

Her brother stood by Rojo's stall, lantern in hand. Judah released Rebecca so quickly the room spun.

"Was that you shooting?" Gabriel asked in a calm tone, his gaze flicking from one to the other.

"Yes, I—" Rebecca began, but Judah interrupted.

"I thought she should know how to shoot," he said, his own voice even. "She's already had one encounter with a rattler. I thought she might feel better if she could fire a gun. I should have asked. I'm sorry."

Gabriel said nothing, but looked from one to the other. Rebecca hoped it was dark enough so he couldn't tell how disheveled they were.

"Beatrice wants you at the house," Gabriel continued in the same tone.

Rebecca drew herself up to tell Gabriel what she thought about that order, but then she glanced at Judah. He was Gabriel's employee, and her retort could reflect on him. She didn't want him to get in trouble on her account. Instead, she nodded, lowered her head, and walked out of the stable without looking back.

CHAPTER
Four

Beatrice stood in the kitchen, her round face creased with anger when Rebecca walked through the door.

"Where have you been?"

"Mr. Merrill was teaching me to shoot. I was afraid to take the children too far because of snakes."

Beatrice's nostrils pinched. "That is not his job, and you shouldn't be taking the children too far in any case. You have no need to know how to shoot. I don't know how to shoot. Your job here is to care for the children. I'm not offering free room and board to a woman who brings scandal upon her family. You have a position here, one you shouldn't neglect, or there will be consequences."

"What consequences? You'll send me back to San Francisco?" Tonight that threat bothered her more than it would have a couple of days ago.

"If I send you back to San Francisco, do you think your father will take you in? He's had enough of you smearing your good name. He'll leave you out on the streets, since your husband didn't see fit to take care of you. Then what?"

She'd fully resigned herself to being a mistress before her exile, and being Neville's mistress had had some appeal. He was young, virile, nice-looking. "I'd manage."

"By becoming a whore for some man?"

Rebecca leaned forward, her temper getting the better of her. "If you think I'm such a horrible person, why do you want me caring for your children?"

"That's enough," Gabriel said quietly, stepping into the kitchen. "I will not have this in my house. Rebecca, you're caring for the children to earn your keep. I do not want these harsh words between you again or I will send you back to San Francisco and let you find a way to support yourself, your soul be damned. Now, go to bed. The children will be up early and will require your attention."

Rebecca wanted to fight back, but was more afraid of what Gabriel would do to Judah than of going back to San Francisco. If she defied him, he might question why she'd gone out alone with Judah, and Judah could suffer for it. This was the life Judah knew, and she couldn't cost him her brother's respect. So she said nothing and went to her room.

―――

Rebecca dangled her bare feet in the water at the creek as she watched the children splash and play. She sat on one of the many flat boulders along the bank, shaded by overhanging trees that made it the perfect escape from Beatrice's watchful eye.

She hadn't slept much last night, partly because she burned for Judah's touch and what she was denied, and partly because she realized she had to make a place for herself in this house, on her own terms. She remembered what Judah had said about keeping the children on a schedule, and giving them chores, so she took them to the garden after breakfast and they pulled weeds. She closed her hand against the pain in her hands, despite her gloves. Granted, her gloves weren't suited for labor such as that, but they were all she had. And her hats certainly weren't appropriate for this blazing sun. She'd never seen the sun burn so long, so many days in a row. She missed the misting San Francisco mornings, the foggy evenings. She was just fine with seeing the sun a few hours a day, if it meant avoiding this heat.

However, between the weed-pulling and playing in the creek, the children were growing too tired to give her mischief. Now, if she could think of something quiet to do with them this afternoon...

She hadn't seen Judah since she left him in the stables last night, and she wondered what Gabriel had said to him, if Judah would dare speak to her again. The idea of losing the one friend she had in this awful place hurt. She'd considered taking the children back to the stable to the kittens, just so she could see him, but if he ignored her, well, she didn't want to deal with that.

Had he lain awake last night thinking about her kisses, the feel of her body against his, the weight of her breast in his hand? And now it was unlikely they'd have a chance to repeat—or continue.

She wanted to slide into the creek with the children and cool her thoughts, but couldn't, not with the responsibility of watching over them. Perhaps she'd come back later, after dark, though every fiber of her being wanted to seek out Judah and go for a ride.

But she couldn't bear for him to reject her, even if it meant saving his job.

That evening, after everyone was in bed, she slipped out of the door near her bedroom and made her way to the creek. The day had cooled, but her skin remained sticky from working in the garden and chasing after the children. Her plan to teach them their letters in the shade of the tree in the yard had been a dismal failure, and she'd spent most of the afternoon trying to keep them out of trouble.

She picked her way to a spot that looked easily accessible, and set the lantern down on a boulder. The water wasn't terribly deep, and was clear as glass as it bubbled over the rocks.

She unbuttoned her shirtwaist, drawing it out of her skirt. Already she felt cooler. What a relief now as she unbuttoned her skirt and let it fall.

Only after she'd removed everything but her chemise did she remember the snake, and she found a branch to hang her skirt and petticoats on. Then, taking a deep breath, she stripped off her chemise and draped it over the rest.

The water was chilly as she placed her foot in it, on the smooth rocks, but the farther she went in, the better the water felt. She went thigh deep, then lowered herself to her knees and sluiced the water over her arms, up her neck, and let her head fall back into the running water, letting it soothe her warm scalp. It wasn't her tub back home, but it was better than standing in the yard and hauling buckets out of the well. She immersed herself completely, looking up at the moon through the clear water. then rose, her hair streaming behind her.

And heard a noise on the bank. She whipped her head toward the sound.

Judah stood beside her clothing, fingering the silk of her chemise. "I never took you for a coward, Rebecca."

She drew her knees in front of her and looped her arms over them, wondering why she made this ridiculous attempt at modesty. "I'm no coward."

"I waited in the stable to take you out on Rojo, but you never came."

He'd waited for her. Relief that her brother hadn't chased him off warmed her, and the truth that she had been a coward, afraid of his rejection, shamed her. Even now they could be making love under the moon. "I didn't want to put your position at risk with Gabriel."

He inclined his head. "I can take care of myself. And if Gabriel wants me gone, I can find another position around here." He crouched on one of the boulders and let his fingers trail in the current. "Probably should have mentioned this is where I take my bath, too."

She swallowed hard, then straightened her legs beneath the water. The night was dark, the moon mostly blocked by the trees, and her body was submerged, but he knew she was naked. What would he do with that knowledge?

"There's plenty of water for both of us," she said boldly.

His hand on her chemise stilled. She dragged her hands through her hair and pushed through her qualms.

"You must be hot after working with the horses all day. The water's lovely."

He moved closer. "I also should have told you predators are likely to come take a drink at night and you shouldn't be alone."

"Are you going to protect me again?"

"I could." He sat on a boulder and removed one boot. "But who's going to protect me?"

She laughed, and he grinned and removed his other boot.

"Are you going to turn around?" he asked when he stood to unbuckle his belt.

She braced her arms behind her on the creek bed. "No."

Again he stilled, as if trying to reason something out, then he shed his pants and stripped off his shirt.

So different than Nathan, so hard, with a lovely vee of dark curling chest hair across his breast, forming a line to his navel and below. She held her breath to see if he would remove his drawers, but he didn't, merely stepped into the creek a few feet away. She stayed beneath the water, but he had to know she was no shy miss, not the way she was watching him, devouring him with her eyes.

He moved past her into the water until it was up to his hips, then bent forward to dip his head in, spraying her with droplets when he straightened again. Then he crouched, three feet away, so the water was up to his shoulders.

"Feels good."

"Yes." The word was breathless as she watched the muscles in his shoulders flex as he moved his arms back and forth under the water.

"Tell me about this scandal that sent you out here," he said, his voice low, husky.

She hesitated, unable to remember the last time she'd cared what someone thought of her. She didn't want to see judgment in his eyes.

"Was it that bad?" he asked, moving a little closer, his fingers brushing against her ankle.

She caught her breath at the seemingly innocent caress. For a moment, she considered fibbing, just so she wouldn't see his disappointment. It wasn't as though he'd learn the truth, unless he asked Gabriel. Her brother would certainly tell, but would Judah ask? Something in his steady gaze prompted her to go with the truth. "I was discovered in an indelicate situation with another man. Quite publicly."

He shifted, and when she looked at him, he had moved closer. Her heart kicked up and her skin tingled. Would he touch her? She wanted him to touch her. When he didn't, she wondered if he thought her as bad as Gabriel and her father did.

"Were you making love to him?"

"No." She would have, later that night, but he hadn't asked that.

"How long since your husband died?"

"Eight months."

"You loved him?"

She hesitated. Had she? "We had a good life. We were—compatible." Especially in bed, in hunger for each other, in their taste for adventure.

"So you don't still mourn him."

The man had left her in an unfavorable position, one where she'd been forced to return to her father's home unless she took the protection of another man. With her reputation, no man would marry her, and she wasn't sure she wanted that again, in any case. "I miss him but don't mourn him."

"That's good to know." He reached out and touched her hair. He drew it over her shoulder, then slipped his hand under it, his rough fingers stroking the back of her neck as he fit his mouth over hers. She welcomed him with a moan, the heat of his mouth, the caress of his tongue, and she lifted her breasts higher, begging for his attention. He didn't accept the offer, merely kept his hand at the back of her neck, his kiss at once sweet and seductive. She lifted her hand to stroke his own hair, thick and wet, and he lowered his hand to curve behind her back, fingers still stroking, drawing heat to his touch and lower. She shifted her legs to relieve the ache between them, wanting him to relieve it. She'd been doing it herself for too long.

He lifted his head and looked down at her for a long moment, his expression unreadable. Was he going to stop? She slid her hand forward to caress the stubble of his cheek, the curve of his ear. He smiled and let his gaze drift to her breasts, white in the moonlight, the peaks tight and dark. "You are a beautiful woman, Rebecca. But I don't want trouble with your brother."

"I have no intention of informing him. Put your hands on me, Judah."

He did, gliding his wet, callused hand up over her breast, weighing it, breathing out as if he was feeling the pleasure she did. She let her head fall back as he plucked her nipple between his fingers. Heat flooded between her legs as he continued the caress, then moved to her other breast, the heel of his hand holding it out of the water. She couldn't stop the gasp of pleasure when he bent his head to sip her nipple between his lips, his stubble caressing the sensitive skin as the water rippled around them. She parted her legs beneath the water, wanting his touch there, too, satisfied to feel the water flow over her wet folds. Eager for the feel of him, she glided her hands over his chest, so different than Nathan, than Neville. A man, not a boy.

Her hunger grew, her curiosity at what making love with him would feel like. Would he continue his gentle seduction, or would he lose control? She suddenly wanted to make him lose control.

She reached beneath the water and found his cock, hard and thick. Her sex swelled in anticipation of feeling him inside her. He jerked a bit at her intimate touch and for a moment, she thought he would break away. But she started stroking, from the base of his shaft to the tip, swirling her thumb over the tip, then repeated the caress, hoping to inspire him to touch her as well. A strangled sound emerged from his throat before he stopped her, closing his hand around her wrist and pulling her hand away. In a rush of water, he rose, lifting her out of the water and onto a nearby boulder. He curved his body over hers, his fingers sliding up her thigh and into the heat of her body without warning. He covered her mouth with his, swallowing her cry. She arched her hips forward, needing his touch deeper as his fingers grew slick with her wetness. His thumb circled over her clitoris, and she spread her legs wider, encouraging his touch, pushing against it, wanting the release he offered her. Sensations pummeled her, his rough fingers, his stubble, his soft lips, the hair of his thighs and chest rubbing over her soft skin.

His touch swirled in a rhythm that made the pleasure tighten deep within her, ready to uncoil, then he changed the rhythm, easing her back from the edge of her orgasm and building her up again. Oh, and she'd worried he might not know how to please her. She'd never been so glad to be wrong.

His fingers moving in and out of her grew wetter with her arousal, and she couldn't remain still under his touch. He lifted himself over her to watch her, and the intensity of his gaze added another level to her pleasure. The combination of his body against hers, his fingers between her legs and the wonder on his face sent her flying.

Too late, he covered his mouth with hers as her cry of release bounced off the water and rocks. The very wantonness of it excited her, and she pushed hard against his thrusting fingers, drawing out the orgasm.

She hadn't floated back to earth before he was lifting her again, carrying her to the bank, laying her down on the soft moss.

He knelt between her parted knees, positioned his cock at her entrance and powered into her still-quivering body.

"Wait. Oh, wait." She closed her hands over his buttocks, holding him inside her, savoring ever sensation—the depth of his penetration, the way he stretched her, the tickle of his hair against her sensitive flesh, the tightness of his strong, hard body against hers, the weight of him over her, the raggedness of his breathing as he held himself back for her. Then she released her grip, and he began to move, in long, measured strokes.

Her fingertips fluttered up his arm that braced him over her, tracing the curves of muscle. She stroked his shoulder and curved her hand over the back of his neck as she lifted into him, matching his strokes, looking into his eyes as they made love. Her arousal built again with each thrust, her body growing wetter around him. His nostrils flared as he moved faster and deeper, the sound of flesh slapping flesh carrying over the sound of the water. She loved the way he filled her with each stroke, the way his thighs hit her backside with every thrust. Intensity lined his face, and she almost wished he would talk to her, tell her what he liked as Nathan had done. But Judah was not Nathan. She would have to learn what pleased him on her own.

Sweat slickened their bodies, and she arched her back and parted her legs wider, so the hair of his groin would rasp her clitoris, which swelled and ached despite its recent attention. Closer, closer, her entire body wound in on itself, ready to spring apart. He pressed deep, holding still to kiss her, his mouth hot and hungry, and she bumped her hips against his, bringing herself to the very edge, needing him to carry her over again. She whimpered, desperate as the sensation eluded her, and he withdrew, only to slide the head of his cock along her slick folds, rubbing against the swollen bundle of nerves once, twice, three times, and she shattered. Her arms dropped to her sides as spirals of pleasure whipped through her body, as he pushed into her body to drive her desire higher, so that even as she was climaxing, her arousal grew. Her body squeezed around his thick length in rhythmic pulses, and he stilled, his own orgasm washing over him, filling her.

And then there was just the sound of his heavy breathing, and hers, as he held himself over her. She threaded her fingers through his chest hair and looked up into his face.

What she saw there gave her pause. "What's wrong?"

"We shouldn't have done that." He withdrew from her and dropped onto his back on the bank beside her, his wrist resting on his forehead, his gaze on the stars above them.

So those stars were real. She thought they might have been part of her orgasm. "We most certainly should have. And should again."

He turned his head to look at her. "I'm a hired hand. You're a lady."

"What difference does that make?"

"You know what difference it makes."

Perhaps if they were going to a ball or a dinner, their social positions would make a difference. But for what just happened here, she didn't see his point. Of course, if she said so, he would get offended. Instead she turned onto her side on the soft grass and smoothed her hand over his chest, feeling the heat of his body, the thundering of his heart.

"This is ours," she said. "No one else's. We aren't anyone here but Rebecca and Judah."

He covered her hand with his and smiled at her. "You are like no woman I've ever met, Rebecca Chatham."

She smiled and rose to lean over him, her breasts rubbing against his chest as she bent to kiss him. "No, I'm not."

Perhaps this exile wouldn't be as painful as she expected.

If Beatrice noticed Rebecca's shadowed eyes the following morning, she didn't say anything. If she noticed her good mood, she didn't comment. After breakfast, Rebecca rounded up the children, marched them out to the garden, where they worked until lunch with occasional breaks beneath a giant oak, then she marched them back to the giant oak with scraps of paper she had gathered from around the house. She was going to teach them their alphabets.

And the fact that the oak had an unimpeded view of the corral where Judah was working a team of horses had absolutely nothing to do with her decision. She watched him behind the pair, getting them used to the harnesses and thinking he was so gentle, so strong, and hers.

The thought surprised her. Hers? Yes, she found him handsome and appealing. Yes, she wanted to repeat their activities from last night as often as possible. But "hers" implied a commitment, a lasting relationship, ownership. She'd owned things, of course, but all of those things were gone now, had lost their meaning, even the gowns she had in storage in the barn.

Besides, how long would she be in exile? Her father would eventually forgive her. She would go home and be a mistress to a wealthy man. She would never marry again. Because while she had owned, she had also been owned, and Nathan's downfall had been her own. Never again.

She redirected David on his task of copying letters and guided Betsy's small hand with her own. When the three of them had copied their names five times, and had copied their alphabet once, Rebecca declared them done and ready for a dip in the creek. They squealed with delight and bolted around the house for the water.

She sat on the very spot where she and Judah had made love, and watched the children play, wishing for night to come.

"You're very adept at slipping out of the house," Judah observed when she entered the barn that evening, skirts sashaying. His pulse kicked. He'd seen her only from afar today, partly a conscious decision. He didn't want to say or do anything improper in front of the children.

She leaned on the stall door beside him, not touching him, focusing on Rojo, not on him. "Gabriel and Beatrice made it easy for me, positioning my sleeping quarters away from the family. They meant to send a message, I'm sure, but it suits me."

"And your maid, Sonia? She doesn't reveal your secrets?"

"She was with me when I was married to Nathan. She has seen much worse."

That wasn't the first time she'd mentioned her marriage in a way that made Judah wonder what kind of marriage she'd had. And the way she'd made love to him last night, her grip on his cock, her eagerness as she took him into her body, as she moved against him, as she came around him, made him wonder, too. It appeared her husband had instructed her well in the ways of lovemaking. He'd lain awake long into the night, remembering her passion. His own wife had been young, and while at first she'd been eager to please him, she hadn't cared for the marriage bed, and sex had been a chore, preparing her, reassuring her, ignoring her discomfort.

He'd had none of that with Rebecca last night. He'd never imagined a lady would be so open, would lie naked on the bank of a creek and wrap herself around him. Would touch him and kiss him, would show him what she liked and take him into her body with such delight.

"Was he good to you, your husband?" he asked, not knowing what else to say.

"We knew how to enjoy ourselves. We had friends and parties and new clothes and fine food and wine. Of course, our tendencies left me with nothing when he died."

"How did he die?"

"In a duel."

Over her honor? Gambling? Dare he ask? "What was the duel about?"

She twirled a loose curl around her finger. "Another man asked to join us in bed. Nathan took offense."

Judah stared. He'd never—well, he'd heard of such a thing, but with a whore, not a married woman. "But you were married."

"And not discreet about our attraction for each other. We were quite scandalous in our attentions. But as you said, we were married, and Nathan was the only man I wanted. Until now." She offered him a smile, but it was sad.

"Do you miss your husband?"

"I do, on occasion. It wasn't a great love, but it was a great passion. I married him against my father's wishes, you know. New wealth, intemperate, young, handsome. My father wanted me to marry a widower with a firm hand to keep me in line. I wanted to marry for love, or what I thought was love at the time."

"Your father didn't disown you?"

"He wasn't happy, and didn't speak to me for almost a year afterwards. It didn't help that he'd receive reports that my husband and I were discovered in indelicate situations in our carriage, or at a ball, or in a garden. But finally he agreed to get to know my husband. He still didn't like him." Her smile grew wistful.

How was he supposed to compare to that, a man who made love to his wife in public places? It seemed Rebecca had enjoyed the attention as well. "And your mother? Did she like him?"

"She passed away when I was twelve. I'm sure that is where I went wrong—I felt I was too old for a governess, and too fast for our housekeeper. I indulged myself in dime novels and decided life should be an adventure."

"You could say this is an adventure," he said.

She turned to face him then, her expression bright. "I could, indeed. Let's saddle Rojo and go for a ride."

He did as she asked, wanting to touch her so badly, wanting to kiss those pretty lips, wanting to feel her against him, wrapped around him. He was like a starving man offered a banquet of his favorite dishes.

He strapped his bedroll to the back of the saddle and saw by the glint in her eyes that she understood. When the horse was saddled, he lifted Rebecca onto Rojo's back and stroked his fingers up the inside of her ankle.

"I'm glad you didn't wear your riding habit," he said as he swung up behind her, then urged Rojo forward, out of the barn.

He didn't tear across the field as he would have liked, as the tension in Rojo's body indicated that he would have liked, as well. Instead he focused on Rebecca's hip against his growing erection, the bare skin of her calf beneath his hand. Letting Rojo have his head, he reached up to unbutton the high neck of Rebecca's blouse, one tiny button at a time. She held her breath as the fabric fell open, revealing her pale skin to the moonlight. She watched his face as he slipped the strap of her chemise down her arm, revealing one perfect breast. He slid his hand over the smooth globe of flesh, rolling her dark tight nipple between his finger and thumb. Her indrawn breath drew his gaze to her face, and he leaned forward to kiss her. Her lips parted for him, her tongue stroked along his lower lip as she twisted her fingers through the hair at the back of his neck. Rojo stepped roughly and her teeth bumped his lip. He drew back with a chuckle and drew her closer against the cradle of his hips, rubbing his erection against her. Hell, if he could, he'd stop the horse now, shove up her skirts and—

No, he'd been too eager last night, hadn't enjoyed her in the way he'd fantasized. He'd enjoyed her, but he'd wanted to spend more time appreciating her lush breasts, kissing every inch of her creamy skin, tasting her arousal.

He grunted and shifted in the saddle. Riding a horse in this state of arousal was not comfortable. But seeing her lips part, her eyelids lower in passion, was worth every jarring bump. He returned his caress to the smooth slope of her breast, then circled his fingertips around her nipple until she held her breath.

Unable to bear the teasing any longer, he pulled up the strap, pulled her blouse into place, and kicked Rojo into a gallop. When they reached the creek where they'd gone two nights before, far enough from the house so that she could scream to the heavens as she came, he slid out of the saddle and pulled her into his arms, body to body, holding her tightly against him as he kissed her, open-mouthed and hungry. She wound her arms around him, pushed her leg between his, her tongue into his mouth and he was dizzy with wanting her. He set her away from him to retrieve his bedroll, and by the time he'd untied it and turned back to her, she'd removed her skirt and blouse, so she stood before him in her shift. He fisted his hands in the bedroll so he wouldn't be tempted to rip the flimsy fabric from her body. Would he ever have self-control while she was near?

Keeping her gaze on his, she drew the garment over her head and stepped out of her drawers, completely naked before him. His cock, already painfully hard, gave an urgent throb. He ignored it, as best he could, and set out the bedroll at the edge of the running water. Then he returned to her, cradled her face in his hands and kissed her mouth, long and slow, at odds with the need pounding through his body. He lowered his mouth to her jaw and her throat. She gasped and clutched his upper arms when he nuzzled the soft skin below her ear, and her nipples speared into his chest through the thin fabric of his shirt. Her legs moved restlessly, so her hips bumped his, rubbing against his erection through his jeans. He slid his hands down her slender back to cup her hips, stilling her, and lowered his mouth to kiss each breast in turn, sucking hard on the tip, pressing it to the roof of his mouth before gentling the caress, then easing farther down her body. She gasped and clutched his head when he rained kisses over her stomach, sliding his touch between her thighs, circling over the smooth flesh until she parted her legs and welcomed his questing fingers.

She was so wet, and her scent filled his head until he couldn't hold off any longer. He urged her legs farther apart and brushed his lips over the curls at the apex of her thighs before delving deeper, sliding his tongue over her cleft, letting her flavor coat his tongue. Her cry of delight rang out and raised gooseflesh on his arms, but he merely cupped her round buttocks in his hands and slid his tongue deeper along her groove. Her flesh quivered against his mouth, hot and pulsing, and he dipped his tongue into her entrance. The moan of delight reverberated through her body and her fingers tightened in his hair.

His name became a soft, urgent chant, and he glided his tongue to flick over her clitoris, circling, stroking, until he felt every muscle in her body tense. He returned his tongue to tease her entrance, then back to the bundle of nerves that swelled even more under his tongue. Up and down, back and forth, licking and kissing and sucking, feeling her growing wetter and wetter, and then she pressed her hips forward with a cry, undulating against him, her flesh under his mouth throbbing.

And then she went boneless. He bore her down to the bedroll and knelt between her legs, covering her mouth with his, wanting to be inside her but, damn it, his impatience had worked against him. He broke away and stripped off his shirt. She leaned forward to help, her fingers tangling with his on his belt buckle. He loved how she laughed. He'd never imagined laughing with a woman during lovemaking.

Then he stopped imagining as she closed her hand around his cock and stroked.

"Inside me," she whispered. "Judah, please, inside me."

He wanted to be naked with her, though everything in him wanted to tumble her onto her back and plow into her. Instead he yanked away and tugged off his boots, shoved down his jeans and dropped over her. She closed her hands in the fabric of his shirt and pulled, baring his chest as he guided himself into her.

She moaned her pleasure as she pushed up against him, bringing him all the way in, pushing his shirt off his shoulders at the same time. Her nails bit into his upper arms as he tunneled into her. Her body gripped him as he dragged himself out of her to drive deeper, like she didn't want him to leave. Her heels rode his ass as he plunged again and again, wanting to lose himself in her. She was so tight, so wet, the curve of her bottom hitting his thighs, her arousal drenching him, her cries urging him on. He bent to slant his mouth over hers, slowing his thrusts. She licked at his mouth and he realized she was tasting herself on his mouth. He felt himself swell, harder than he'd ever been, and he broke the kiss, reluctantly, to power into her again.

But it wasn't enough. He wrapped his arms around her back and sat on his heels, drawing her with him, over him, gravity pushing him deeper into her body. She gasped, her hair falling over her shoulders toward him as she clutched his shoulders and rode him, pounding against him, taking him deeper than he thought possible. She grabbed his hand and guided it between them to her clitoris.

"Touch me, Judah. Take me back."

Never had a woman told him how to please her. He brushed his thumb over the swollen knot. She pushed down hard, going still, her channel pulsing around him as he stroked, her breath coming faster and faster, and then she held it, held him prisoner as he flicked his thumb up and down, up and down. Then she released her breath in a long, keening cry, her pussy squeezing him, her head falling back in release. He wanted to let her ride it out, but his body demanded more. He pushed up into her, his thighs burning, his balls tight and aching, all that liquid heat convulsing on his cock. He gripped her hips and pulled her down on him, holding her close, pushing into her as deep as he could get before exploding inside her, the orgasm rocketing through him.

God, nothing like it, soft woman all around him, her hair falling over his sensitive skin, her soft sighs washing over his skin as she dropped her head to his shoulder. Still inside her, still weak with his climax, breathing heavy with it, he lowered her onto the bedroll. He stroked her hair back from her face and rose enough to look into her eyes.

No, he'd never known another woman like her.

Reluctantly, he withdrew and dropped onto his back beside

her. He wished she'd roll onto her side and play with his chest hair as she'd done last time, but instead she lay with her hand flung over her head, staring at the stars and catching her breath.

"Is the sky like this in Montana?" she asked, turning her head toward him.

God, she was gorgeous, naked in the moonlight, not self-conscious at all about her body, though why would she be? She was perfect.

And she wanted to talk about his past. Even through his orgasm-hazed brain, he could reason that out.

"It's like this," he said cautiously.

"But cold, you said. So you don't swim much in the creek?"

"Not cold all the time. We get some scorchers in the summer. But the winters are hell on man and beast." He turned onto his side to face her. "Are you telling me you want to go swim in the creek?"

"Maybe before we head back. I want to know about your life before."

"It's not something I care to talk about." Especially after making love to her.

"Were you a foreman out there?" she pressed anyway.

"My family owned some land. I worked on it, as we all did."

"All? Brothers and sisters?"

A smile tugged at his lips at her curiosity. "Two brothers and a sister."

"But you chose to strike out on your own instead of stay there."

"My father and I didn't see eye to eye, especially after my wife died. So, yes."

"What was her name?" Her face brightened at the mention of his wife. Clearly this was the information she'd been after.

"Elizabeth. She was much younger, afraid of everything, and died of fever." That was all the information he wanted to share with her.

"Did you love her?"

How would he answer that? If he answered truthfully, would she think him heartless? But he'd asked her the same about her husband, and she'd been honest.

"It was an arranged marriage. Her father's land was nearby and my family wanted a dynasty. That ended with her death. Or at least for my part. I left when they wanted me to marry her sister weeks after burying Elizabeth. I didn't look back."

A frown furrowed her brow. "Marry her sister? Even if you didn't love her, that would have been hard."

"They wanted a child to seal the bond. I couldn't be part of that. So I'm going to make my own way." He stroked her hair back from her face, wanting to end this unpleasant memory, especially when he was happier now with her than he'd ever been. "Let's go for that swim."

The days passed too slowly for Rebecca, though she did manage to get the children into a routine as he'd suggested. She'd even taken the time to write down stories she remembered from childhood to read to them, since Beatrice didn't have any books at all. Even scrounging up paper was a challenge. She illustrated some of the books with pictures that made the children laugh and want to draw their own.

They'd spend the afternoon in the creek. Sonia had fashioned a decent bathing suit for her out of one of her least-favorite dresses so that she could go into the water with the children. And she was pleasantly surprised when David offered her a spontaneous hug one night before bed.

Every night, she'd slip out of the house and down to the stable where Judah and Rojo waited. Every night, they made love under the stars. As Rebecca grew to know him better, she showed him some of the games she and Nathan had played in bed. She showed him how pleasurable it was for him to take her from behind, or how erotic it was for them to masturbate in front of each other. They tried to make love while standing against a tree, but the bark was too rough. Her skin still bore the scratches.

They talked, too, while lying in each other's arms, about why he chose California and how he was so good with horses. He wanted to own his own place nearby and do nothing but train horses. He was saving money for that goal. She didn't ask if he saw a family in that future. Of course a man like him would want a family. But since she didn't, she didn't bring it up.

He'd ask her about San Francisco and she told him about the parties and theater and fashion. She missed dressing up and wearing a hat that did absolutely no good and wearing shoes that she didn't have to worry about dirtying, and while she didn't miss wearing a corset, she missed the figure it gave her.

Then he proceeded to show her he found nothing wrong with her figure.

Dawn was breaking as they rode Rojo back home one morning. They'd become more and more bold about staying out the past few nights. Rebecca was stiff from a night spent on the ground, deliciously achy from making love three times, but she nestled under his chin. Her imagination might be playing tricks on her, but he seemed to be sitting higher in the saddle. Male pride made her smile, and she nuzzled against his chest.

"Red sky in the morning—we'll have rain later," he murmured as they crested the rise above the house.

Lazily she scanned the scene below. No activity on the ranch, no hands about, no one tending to the animals. She hadn't realized she was worried about it until her stomach relaxed. What would happen if she was caught, anyway? Would her brother send her back to San Francisco? No, but he might let Judah go. She had to be careful for his sake.

Reluctantly, it seemed, Judah let her off Rojo in front of the door leading to her room. She smiled up at him, then ducked inside, winding her hair back into place. As she slipped into her room, she heard a door open down the hall.

Sonia lifted her head from her pillow and frowned. "Where have you been?"

Rebecca placed her finger to her lips, then jumped as a knock sounded on the door just behind her head. She smoothed her skirt, her hair, then turned to open the door. Beatrice stood there, her eyes narrowed.

"Did I just hear your door close?"

"Yes, I was going out to get some water to wash up, but I forgot my wrap." She snatched a shawl from the end of the bed.

"It isn't cold."

"It was to me." She folded the fabric around herself, though Beatrice was right. The morning had been steamy, which evidenced what Judah had said about rain.

Beatrice didn't move. Neither did Rebecca.

"Is there something else?"

"No. Breakfast will be ready at the usual time."

Rebecca frowned. Clearly Beatrice expected to find something out of the ordinary. What had aroused her suspicion?

―――

"You were wrong about the rain," Rebecca said as she strolled into the barn that night, her heart kicking as it did every time she saw Judah. She'd wanted to see him all day, but didn't trust herself around him with the other cowhands were around.

He grunted as he tightened the cinch around Rojo's belly. "It was a purely miserable day, though."

The air had been heavy, and the dampness had kept the children sluggish, so Rebecca hadn't minded, especially since she hadn't had much sleep last night. She moved closer and twined her hand through the reins, an idea forming in her mind. Would he agree?

When he placed his hands on her waist to lift her into the saddle, she leaned forward and let her mouth cover his, slipping her tongue between his surprised lips, just briefly, before she let herself be raised.

A nice breeze was blowing when they reached the creek, the first Rebecca had felt all day, and she lifted her face to it, releasing her hair from its pins so it trailed behind her like a flag. Judah laid out the bedroll and held a hand to her. She stepped toward him, then stopped.

"I'd like to do something."

He angled his head, his eyes narrowed. "What?" he asked warily.

Perhaps she had pushed things too far the other night when she'd taken his balls into her mouth while caressing the sensitive skin behind them. He'd climaxed with a shout, so he hadn't actually minded, though he'd squirmed a bit.

"Give me your belt."

He eased back. "The last time someone asked me to do that, I got a whipping."

"I promise not to do that." She knew some people did enjoy it as part of sex play, though she had never seen the appeal.

Slowly, keeping his gaze on hers, he unbuckled the belt, drew it from his belt loops and handed it to her. She stretched it between her hands, testing its pliability, then walked behind him. He turned his head to follow her progress.

"Put your hands behind you and fold them together," she said.

Again reluctant, he did as she instructed. She sank to her knees and wrapped the leather around his strong wrists, pulling it tight, and wrapping it again before looping the end through his linked hands and tugging. His breathing grew ragged as she rose and stood in front of him. Slowly, she unbuttoned her blouse and let it hang open over her shift as she unfastened her skirt and let it fall to the ground. She stepped out of it, let her blouse float to rest on top of it, then bent over slowly, so her chemise fell open, to remove her boots. She looked up to see him staring at her breasts through the gap in the fabric, and straightened.

"Do you want to touch me?"

"Yes," he said through clenched teeth.

"Wait." She pulled the chemise over her head and let it rest on the other clothes, then slowly slid down her drawers, then straightened, standing before him in the moonlight diffused by the clouds overhead. She slid her hands up her waist to cup her breasts, rubbing her thumbs over her hard nipples, and watched his eyes glint in desperate hunger. Just that, the way he was looking at her like he wanted to devour her, excited her, and she felt a surge of wetness between her legs. Though she wanted to move quickly, she was doing this for his pleasure as well, and trailed her fingertips down the center of her body to her mons. She stroked the hair there before widening her stance and slipping her hand between her thighs.

He made a strangled sound, and the tendons in his neck tightened.

She smiled and trailed her wet fingers up her belly, swirling them around her navel before dipping back between her legs. The way he watched the movement of her hand made her wetter, and she dipped a finger inside herself, then lifted her hand to her lips.

"Rebecca."

She smiled, glossed her lips with her juices, then bent to let him lick her mouth. He surged forward, but was off balance with his hands bound behind him. She straightened him, then reached down to unbutton his pants, bringing his erection free. She hadn't thought this all the way through, because undressing him would be nearly impossible in this position. Instead, she pulled his cock free and stroked up and down, using the wetness from her own body to lubricate her caresses as he struggled to hold back his groans. She stepped back, returned her caresses to her own breasts, then knelt before him. She opened his shirt, trailing kisses down his chest as she did, nuzzling his chest hair. She then let her hair fall forward, teasing his erection, before she closed her hand around it and guided it to her mouth. His salty, musky flavor filled her mouth as she stroked the swollen head, flicked her tongue along the slit before sliding it down along the underside, tracing the pulsing vein.

"Rebecca, sweet God, you have to—" he groaned, even as he lifted his hips to push his cock farther into her mouth.

She parted her lips over his member and took him deeper, until the tip of him tapped the back of her throat, and then she slid back up, then down again in the rhythm of sex. His muscles tightened all over.

"I need to be inside you, Rebecca, damn it."

She stroked him twice more, up and down, her fingers wrapped around the base of his cock, squeezing, pumping, and then she sat back to look up at him.

"Do you want me to ride you?"

"Untie me," he growled. "I need to fuck you."

Delight washed through her. He'd said the word once or twice, but not with such need in his voice, and she reached behind him to loosen the leather.

The next thing she knew, she was on her back, her hands pinned beside her head, and he speared into her, hard, rough, out of control as he pounded into her.

"So wet," he managed. "You make me crazy, Rebecca. So…damn…good."

She loved how he held her down, how he powered over her. She lifted her legs to tuck her knees beneath his armpits, opening herself to him, bringing him deeper with each thrust that slammed into her tender flesh. She tightened her body around him each time he pulled out, and he hissed his approval before driving back into her. He released her hands to cup under her bottom, holding her, rolling against her, the hair above his cock rubbing against her swollen clitoris, the thick flesh stroking magical places inside her, her wetness coating both of them.

"Come," he ordered, holding her buttocks apart so he could push deeper. "Come, Rebecca." Thrusting harder. "Come."

Her body, coiling tighter with each command, flew apart when his thumb swept over her swollen flesh, and continued circling as he thrust shallowly in her body. She arched against him, wanting him to fill her as she flew, and he followed her, plunging deep, staying there so she could feel the ripples along his cock as he emptied into her.

He dropped to the bedroll beside her and pulled her close.

"You're a wicked woman," he said, pressing a kiss to her hair. "I can't get enough of you."

The sky illuminated briefly, and she lifted her head, just as a rumble of thunder shook the ground beneath them.

"There's your rain," she said, kissing his chest, though he still wore his shirt.

He grunted and pulled free. "We'd better get back."

She whimpered in protest when he tossed her her chemise.

"You don't want to go into the house drenched."

But even as he said it, the first drops began to fall, big fat ones, splashing on her face, in the dirt. Squealing, she snatched her clothes up before they became muddy, and he gathered the bedroll, probably grateful he hadn't undressed. She fastened her skirt and shrugged into her blouse as he soothed a restless Rojo. The rain was pouring in earnest when Judah reached for her to help her into the saddle. She wrapped her arms around his shoulders and pressed her mouth to his. He tightened his arms around her and slanted his mouth, accepting her kiss, deepening it as the rain washed over them, plastering their clothes to them. He buried his hand in her heavy hair, angling her head as he devoured her mouth. She rubbed her body along his and felt his cock growing hard again. She captured his hand and dragged it to her breast, where he kneaded it through the thin fabric. She eased back just a bit to look into his eyes, saw the desire there.

"In the rain," she whispered. "Please, Judah."

He turned her around. "Hold onto the saddle."

She did as he asked, feeling the heat of Rojo's body as she leaned forward and Judah lifted her skirts. He parted her buttocks with a quick caress, then guided himself into her. The position was precarious, so he couldn't go fast, which only made each slide of his cock in her channel that much better. Slow, steady, each thrust making her sex swell and ache. He stroked her breasts through her wet chemise as the rain poured down on them, as the thunder rumbled. Then he held her hips, pumping a little faster, driving her desire higher, his wet jean-clad thighs slapping against her bare ones. Rojo shied at a clap of thunder, but gentle words from Judah calmed him and he stilled. Then Judah slid his touch around to her clitoris, his hand wet with rain and her juices, and she came undone, thrusting her hips back into him as her entire body unraveled. He stilled her hips and thrust harder into her quivering body until he, too, came with a grunt of satisfaction.

He pressed his face against her back, between her shoulders, for a moment as they caught their breath. Then he withdrew and smoothed down her skirt.

"We need to go. The lightning is getting closer."

He lifted her into the saddle, which wasn't all that comfortable after being made love to twice. He mounted right behind her, curved his body over hers and kicked Rojo into a gallop. The big horse skidded in the mud a few times, and lost his rhythm so that Judah had to hold onto Rebecca tightly. She could feel his heart thudding in time with the horse's hooves but she wanted to throw her head back and laugh.

The storm raged over them as they entered the stable, where the other horses were restless, as well. They hadn't been gone more than two hours, so it was still early, and a few of the other cowhands were in the barn. They looked at Judah and Rebecca curiously and she glanced down to ensure she'd closed her blouse.

"I'll see you to the house," he said as he reached for her.

"Never mind that. You need to see to Rojo."

She wanted to kiss him good night as they always did, but they had too many witnesses. So she smiled instead and hurried away.

Beatrice was in the kitchen when Rebecca entered the hallway by her bedroom. Beatrice turned and her eyes widened to see Rebecca's bedraggled state.

"Where have you been?"

"I went for a ride."

"A ride? Dressed like that?"

"My riding habit is too hot."

"We don't have side saddles."

"Mr. Merrill showed me how to ride with my knee over the pommel."

Beatrice approached. "Mr. Merrill. Did he go with you?"

Rebecca felt her face heat and hoped Beatrice didn't notice in the dim light. "Of course he did. Otherwise I'd get lost."

"Without a chaperone."

Rebecca squared her shoulders. "Why would I need a chaperone, Beatrice? This isn't San Francisco, after all. We don't have to worry about appearances, do we?"

Beatrice drew back, inspecting her sister-in-law. "You might think about what others would say if they knew you were riding about the countryside alone with a hired man."

Hired man. Was that what Beatrice worried about? Or Rebecca's reputation? Rebecca couldn't let herself care.

"I'm going to get out of these wet clothes. Though I admit it feels good to be cool after today. Good night, Beatrice." She kept her hand on the door meaningfully until Beatrice finally turned away. Then she closed the door and leaned against it, wondering why on earth she cared what Beatrice thought.

―――

The following morning, Rebecca waited for Beatrice to mention something about Rebecca's ride to Gabriel, but her sister-in-law had something else on her mind.

"We need to leave around noon to get to the Raymond's ranch," she said. "I worked late last night getting everything packed. Rebecca, you need to get the children's best clothes packed, and they need to dress in their second best."

"We need to leave earlier than that after the rain last night. The roads will be mud."

"I took that into account when I planned our schedule."

"Where is it we're going?" Rebecca asked, at a loss.

"The Raymonds' eldest daughter is getting married and they've invited all the neighbors to the celebration."

"Neighbors being relative," Gabriel said. "It's over two hours away on the best day."

Rebecca's stomach sank. "So we won't be back tonight." No ride with Judah, no lying in his arms. Being with him was the best part of the day. Could it be—no. She hadn't fallen in love with him. She just looked forward to spending the best part of the day with him. That wasn't love. It was anticipation. And joy. And… oh, dear.

Beatrice cast an annoyed glance in her direction. Apparently the other woman had still been talking while Rebecca's mind had tried to wrap around this revelation.

"No, we'll camp there and head back in the morning. You have camped before?"

Not outside. She shook her head.

Beatrice's eyes lit with satisfaction. "You'll have to make do tonight. Now, get the children ready."

Still numb from the realization that she was in love, and wondering what on earth she would do about it, Rebecca silently went to do Beatrice's bidding. At least she'd have time away from him to work it all out.

———

Rebecca's pulse picked up when she walked outside to help the children into the carriage. Judah was helping Gabriel hook up the team, and Rojo was saddled nearby.

"Are you going with us?" she asked as she moved to lift Vernon into the carriage.

Judah reached past her for the boy and swung him in, his arm brushing hers. "I'll be riding alongside in case anything goes wrong. We have enough hands here to hold the place down until morning." He cast her a sideways smile.

Yesterday that smile wouldn't have made her blush, but this morning she felt her whole body warm. She wanted to lean into him, and because of that, took a step in the opposite direction.

"I thought the carriage wasn't suitable for the roads around here, especially after last night's rain," she said, loud enough for her brother to hear.

"Beatrice won't travel any other way," Gabriel said without looking at her as he gave the harness one final tug.

The woman herself came out then, a valise in hand, wearing a lovely traveling dress that was too tight and no doubt too hot in the humidity after last night's storm. Gabriel handed her into the front seat.

"Let me just get my bag," Rebecca said, heading toward the house.

"We don't have time," Beatrice said.

"I'm packed." Thanks to Sonia, who would be staying behind, since there was no room in the carriage. Honestly, if Rebecca hadn't had to care for the children, she was sure she would be left behind, too. She wondered if it had occurred to Beatrice to leave the children with Rebecca. She certainly wouldn't mention it, now that Judah was going along. "It will only take me a moment."

Beatrice huffed, and Rebecca hurried inside. When she emerged, the carriage was already turned toward the road.

"Sit in back with the children," Beatrice instructed. "Gabriel, you need to put the top up."

"The team doesn't like the top up," he said. "Let me get them on the road first, then I'll get it up."

"My skin cannot bear this sun," Beatrice countered.

The woman was in the garden every day with no more protection than a straw hat smaller than the one she currently wore, but Rebecca kept her mouth shut, though she caught Judah's amused glance and returned a smile of her own. Likely the woman was sweltering in the warm jacket. Her face was certainly florid. If Gabriel put the top up, it would offer shade, yes, but would capture the heat in the back seat and make the ride miserable for Rebecca and the children. Rebecca wore her new uniform of shirtwaist and skirt, but she suspected Beatrice had to put on a corset to get into her clothing.

"Do you think we'll get more rain today?" Rebecca asked her brother. The clouds were clearing, but the moisture in the air was so thick she could almost drink it.

"No telling. Likely."

"That would be awful for the poor Raymonds, to be planning this wedding only to have it rain!" Beatrice exclaimed.

And their guests would be camping outside. Rebecca gave a delicate shudder. She hoped they would have tents at the very least.

Beatrice got her way, and the shade was pulled up on the carriage, leaving Rebecca and the children to swelter in the back, and their vision limited to what was in front of them. Judah, of course, rode beside them. She could hear him but not see him. And goodness, she loved to watch him ride, his lean body loose in the saddle, moving with the horse's gait. She felt her face heat again as she remembered the night she'd ridden out facing him, her skirts up, letting Rojo's steps create the friction between her sex and Judah's cock. They'd been panting and frantic when they reached the creek, barely able to get each other's clothes off, coming almost the moment he thrust inside her.

Well. That was certainly an inappropriate memory to have while riding with her family. She swallowed and turned her attention to the children who, unable to see over the seat back, and ignored by their parents, became restless. Rebecca had expected as much, since they could barely sit at the table for fifteen minutes without fidgeting. She drew out the books she'd made and began to read with them. Betsy climbed onto her lap, which only made her hotter, but she didn't set the child aside. Instead, she pointed to each word as she read it. Betsy had heard the story of the three bears often enough that she could finish Rebecca's sentences for her. The swaying of the carriage and the heat lulled the little girl and Vernon to sleep, and David took one of her books to read on his own. Rebecca leaned against the side of the carriage and watched the scenery.

They got stuck in the mud a few times, but Judah and Gabriel were able to dislodge them. And by mid-afternoon, they arrived at the Raymonds'.

Rebecca had forgotten what it was like to be around a crowd of people. After she helped the children out of the carriage, she stood and scanned her surroundings. Two dozen carriages and wagons were parked, maybe more. Tables were set up close to the two-story house that was twice as big as Gabriel's. People gathered in groups around the tables, talking and laughing, probably less accustomed than she to socializing. Beatrice hurried to join them, leaving Gabriel and Judah to tend to the horses and Rebecca to the children.

Once she'd situated the children by finding them playmates to occupy their time, her brother approached with her valise.

"You'll want to change for the wedding. I believe the ladies have a spot in the house."

She thanked him and turned to go.

"Rebecca."

She stopped and looked over her shoulder at him.

"Those stories—I remember Mother telling them to us when we were young. Thank you for sharing them with my children. You're very good with them."

Before she could recover herself to respond, he disappeared into the crowd.

She found the room designated for the female guests to change. Beatrice was already there, already changed, and for the second time in ten minutes, Rebecca was speechless.

Beatrice had shoved her body into one of Rebecca's ball gowns, a green moire that did nothing to enhance Beatrice's coloring. She'd altered it, certainly, but there wasn't enough fabric to make it much larger, and Beatrice was squeezed into the abomination. Before Rebecca could check herself, she strode toward her sister-in-law and grabbed her arm. The fabric nearly squeaked in protest, it bound her flesh so tightly.

"What are you doing with my gown?"

Beatrice lifted her chin, but also sent a glance about the room, no doubt concerned about what the other women were thinking. "You weren't using it. It was sitting in the barn. I didn't think you'd miss it."

Rebecca understood that Beatrice didn't have money or nice clothes, but, "You didn't ask? Did you not think I'd recognize it, even with the alterations?"

"Would you have said yes?"

After she'd laughed herself silly? She may not have. She didn't like that realization about herself, and released her sister-in-law's arm. Still. "It's common courtesy. The dress is mine."

"And you live in my house. By my good will. Giving me this dress is the least you can do."

"I take care of your children while you pretend they don't even exist," Rebecca countered.

"You are working for me because your father sent you away because you were whoring yourself!"

Rebecca backed away, aware of the gasps of distress from the ladies surrounding them. But she didn't move away from shame. She moved away because she feared she might do violence to the other woman.

Beatrice's expression smoothed into a look of triumph as Rebecca felt her face heat. She wanted to escape, but doing so would admit guilt. She wouldn't give Beatrice the satisfaction. Pride and defiance surging through her—always a combination that got her into trouble--she unfastened her skirt and let it fall, then unbuttoned her blouse and stood before the ladies in her shift, letting them see she wore no corset, before she bent to open her valise. She unfolded her favorite gown, a peacock-blue silk with a cuirasse bodice that dipped low in front and in back, hugged her torso to her hips and left her arms bare. The skirt formed a v-shape and fell in tucks beyond that, though it gathered in the back. It had always reminded her of a mermaid. She didn't know if she could get into it without a corset, but she was going to try.

She stepped into the skirt and drew a deep breath before fastening it at her waist, then slid her arms into the bodice and managed the bottom few buttons on her own. Oh, dear. She would not ask Beatrice for help, and Sonia had not come. Fortunately, one of the other ladies saw her dilemma and stepped forward. Rebecca held her breath until the last button was fastened, then turned to smile her appreciation to the woman. She stood regally in the center of the room, a definite peacock among the country hens.

And she felt ashamed of herself for wanting to show off.

"I'll just go see to my hair," she said, bending at the knees to scoop up her valise and escape.

Judah straightened from leaning against the wall when Rebecca walked out of the house, head held high, valise in hand. She was a sight in a gown that glimmered in the sunlight, that pushed up her breasts and hugged her slim waist. But her expression didn't match the beauty of her dress, and when he approached, he saw tears in her eyes.

"What is it?" he asked, taking her arm and leading her around the side of the house, where no one could see them.

She shook her head and swallowed hard. "Nothing at all. I need to change my shoes and I don't think I can bend over."

"I'll do it." He crouched before her, pawed through her valise until he came up with two shoes that would be ruined in the dirt here. "You look like an angel."

"Or a devil," she choked.

He snapped his gaze to her face and saw she was trying not to cry. "Did Beatrice say something?" he asked as he unlaced her boots and removed them gently, one at a time.

She shook her head. "Well, she did, but I'm more ashamed of my response. Why did I think this was a proper thing to wear to a wedding?"

He stroked a rough hand lightly over the fabric. He'd never touched anything so soft, except her skin. "Because it's a beautiful gown."

"But we're here in the middle of nowhere. My pride, Judah. I knew no one else here would have something this grand, and I chose to wear it anyway. What kind of person am I?"

He straightened and closed his hands over her arms, forcing her to look at him. The tears swimming in her eyes were almost his undoing. "You're a beautiful woman who is used to being the center of attention. Just because you're far from home doesn't mean that's changed."

Something flashed in her eyes before she averted her gaze, focusing on his shoulder. "I don't even know these people. What must they think of me, after they invited me to this wedding?"

"Would you rather change back into your traveling clothes? Because you're never going to blend in, Rebecca."

He'd meant it as a compliment, but the way she flinched, one would have thought he'd struck her.

"I would like to change back into my traveling clothes, yes," she said, pulling away. "I'll see if I can get someone to help me."

He stopped her by placing a hand against the wall, blocking her escape. He didn't understand exactly what had her so upset, but he was determined to set her to rights. "I can help you." Though it would be a shame to remove this lovely gown.

She glanced about, then motioned to the back of the house, where she turned her back to him to unbutton the shiny, tiny black buttons. His hands shook only a little with longing to stroke the pale skin he bared, but he resisted. When the garment was loose, she let it fall down her arms and pulled her wrinkled blouse from her valise and put it on, smoothing it the best she could against her waist before changing out of her skirt. When she was dressed, she turned to him, fluffing her hair about her shoulders, though she still had tears in her eyes.

"Shall we go witness the ceremony?" he asked, not knowing what else to say.

"I'll put this in the carriage and join you."

He let her go because he thought she needed time to gather herself. But she didn't join him as the wedding started. When he saw her again, after the ceremony, held under a flowered arbor at one end of the yard, she was standing in the back with the children, her beautiful face smooth, but her eyes shadowed and her lush lips down-turned, such a change from the woman he'd come to know. But when he moved to join her, she turned away.

After a lavish spread of barbecued beef and all manner of side-dishes provided by the neighbor ladies, the band began to play. The bride and groom—both so young and happy it hurt to look at them—moved to the center of the yard and turned into each other's arms, smiling as if they were alone in the world. Right now, Judah wanted Rebecca in his own arms, looking up at him just like that.

Others joined the bridal couple, their parents, other neighbors. Gabriel and his wife held back, though Beatrice sat forward, her hands pressed together, clearly longing to dance. And there was Rebecca, on the floor with David, her hand on his shoulder, head bent as he solemnly stepped as she instructed, his hand on the waist of her muddy skirt. Judah had to watch them for a moment, the sweetness of the scene, before he approached.

"Mind if I cut in, young David?" he asked, giving the young man a cursory glance before turning his gaze to Rebecca.

David started to turn away, but Rebecca gently caught his

hand, showed him how to hand her off to Judah, and then allowed him to escape to play with his friends.

"Did I interrupt a lesson?" Judah asked, placing his hand at her waist and drawing her just a bit closer than was proper.

"We shouldn't be doing this," she said, a blush touching her cheeks, making her even prettier.

"Why not?"

She swayed toward him as if she couldn't help herself, then forced herself straight. "People will know."

That irritated him, though he couldn't say why. Maybe because the woman he'd gotten to know over the past few weeks didn't care what others thought, and if they thought something, hell, she adjusted. "You're the only woman I know here, outside of Beatrice, and I'm the only one you know outside of your brother. And why do you care if they know?"

"What do you think Gabriel will do to you if he knows about us?"

He lifted his head at that. "I'll land on my feet just fine."

"But you're working toward having your own place."

"And if I have to start that earlier than planned, I'll be fine." He cupped his hand over her cheek and forced her gaze to his. "I'll be fine."

She looked into his eyes a moment, then nodded, a small smile fluttering her lips. He dropped his hand from her face and drew her closer to turn her in a sweeping move. Her laugh carried over the sound of the music and several heads turned in their direction. And he'd been right about the way she felt in his arms, once she relaxed. Perfect. Now that she wasn't worried about what others thought, she was looking at him just the way the bride was looking at her groom. For the first time in a long time, he began to wonder if he could start over.

Would Rebecca be a rancher's wife? What he'd seen today showed her maybe she could.

After a few songs, he stepped back and took her hand. "Come with me."

She glanced about. Her brother and his wife were dancing, the children were piled sleepily on a blanket. She smiled at him and followed. He led her to the corner of the house, where he'd helped her out of her dress, and drew her into his arms, his fingers resting lightly on her jaw. He wanted to tell her he loved her, wanted to discover if she felt the same way. But she looped her arm around his neck and stretched up to kiss him.

He lost himself in the sweetness of her for a moment, in the softness of her. Of course she would think that was why he'd brought her back here, but he had no intention of making love to her, not with all these people around. But he couldn't resist just a moment more of feeling her tongue slide along his, her hand glide over his chest, her breath wash over his cheek. But memories of the past nights in her arms overrode common sense, and he eased her back against the wall. She giggled against his mouth—God, he loved how she laughed when they were together, and he curved his hands over her ribs, just under her breasts. He quelled the urge to fill his palms with their weight, but took the kiss deeper.

"What on earth is going on here?" a shrill voice proclaimed behind them, and Rebecca stiffened in his arms.

He lifted his head and turned to see Beatrice and Gabriel standing behind them, Beatrice with her hands on her hips.

CHAPTER
Five

Rebecca sat straight-spined in the kitchen of the Raymonds' home, Beatrice standing before her in the stolen dress, her arms crossed so that the seams threatened to split. Gabriel stood quietly behind her, and Judah was nowhere in sight. The knot in her stomach was worse than it had been in her father's study in San Francisco. This time her impulses affected others, and while Judah had said their dalliance wouldn't adversely affect him, she'd realized she didn't know her brother well enough to know that to be true.

"What were you thinking, showing such a display out there?" Beatrice demanded through clenched teeth. "Have you no thought for my reputation? What must these people think about the kind of house I run? The kind of woman who cares for my children?"

Rebecca wanted to point out that no one would have known she'd been in Judah's embrace if Beatrice hadn't made such a scene. And it seemed to her no one really cared that the governess and the foreman were caught kissing behind the house, no matter how intimate. But her throat closed as she waited to hear the fate of Judah. Would she see him again? If she was sent back to San Francisco, she certainly wouldn't. His life was here.

"I cannot believe you humiliated me in front of our friends

with your wild behavior. I think—your brother and I need to talk about your future in our home."

Rebecca kept her chin high. She wouldn't chance a glance at her brother, afraid he would recognize her fear.

"Is there anything else?"

Beatrice huffed. "It's too late to go home tonight. We have to endure the humiliation and gossip for a few more hours, at least. But you will sleep tonight where I can see you, since I can see now that you've been riding out with him so he can put his hands on you."

Rebecca's face heated, and she rose, her shoulders tight. "I'll see to the children."

"You needn't bother. I don't want you near them."

That hurt more than she expected. She nodded and moved past her brother and out the door.

There was some attention when she walked out, but people didn't seem as scandalized as Beatrice. And Judah was nowhere in sight. She wondered if she dared to go to the stable, or if Beatrice would erupt. Suddenly, she didn't care. What would Beatrice do to her? Rebecca picked up her skirts and hurried toward the stables.

But Rojo was gone.

Panic was chased quickly by anger and she whirled to go look for her brother. He must have seen her expression, because he moved away from the group of men he was talking to and intercepted her.

"Did you send him away?" she demanded, using the very last of her resources to stop herself from shoving his chest as she had when she was a child.

"What?"

"Judah. Did you send him away? Are you letting him go?"

"What are you talking about?"

"Judah's gone. Did you tell him he wouldn't be working for you anymore? Because if you did, you're making a huge mistake. He's the best cowboy you've got. He cares about the animals. He wants to make something of himself. And all that, what you saw, that was my fault. I was bored, and I seduced him. He shouldn't be punished for my sins."

Gabriel's forehead creased further. "He's left?"

"Rojo is gone, and I don't see him." She drew back, understanding dawning. "You didn't send him away?" He'd left on his own. Why? To protect her? Or to escape her?

"I didn't send him away."

"You don't intend to." It wasn't quite a question.

"I hadn't thought—I would think your humiliation here would be enough to keep you apart. If not, I will have to make other considerations. He is beneath you, Rebecca."

She opened her mouth to give a saucy retort, but his reddened cheeks told her he reached that observation on his own. "I love him."

She wasn't sure who was more surprised by the admission—herself or her brother. He recovered first, grabbed her arm, and drew her farther from the crowd. His expression when he turned back to her was not the judgmental one he'd worn in the kitchen when he'd been at Beatrice's side. No, it was more a gentle exasperation, like he didn't know what to do with her, but couldn't hate her.

"What exactly has been going on between the two of you?"

His tone matched his face, and surprised her into honesty. "He's been my only friend here, and my lover these past weeks."

Gabriel shook his head. "Thinking it would go where? That he would marry you? He's a poor man, a cowboy. Father would never allow it. I would never allow it. And you allowed him to dishonor you?"

"There is no dishonor in love, Gabriel."

"Is that what you said about your husband? When he used you so publicly and left you with nothing? Do you want that again?"

She wouldn't flinch from his words. What she and Judah had wasn't like her marriage to Nathan. Everything had been a challenge to Nathan. Judah was content to be with her. "Judah makes me happy."

"You have only known him a matter of weeks, just as it was with Nathan." He shook his head and backed away. "Our father trusted me with this task, and I failed him. I failed you. I'll send you back as soon as I can spare the wagon to get you to the train."

She swayed back, away from him, her heart dropping. When she returned to San Francisco, she would never see Judah again.

―――

The ride back to the ranch the next day was miserable. Rebecca was hot and dirty and tired—she hadn't slept at all on the hard ground a few feet from Beatrice. And Beatrice had insisted that Rebecca ride in the front with Gabriel, as if she didn't want Rebecca near her children. Rebecca was only slightly gratified that David cried for her and wanted a story, only to be hushed by Beatrice. So it was a long and quiet journey.

And Judah wasn't at the ranch, either, though she wasn't allowed to seek him out, ushered into the house instead.

Rebecca washed in the meager water Sonia had fetched for her, but it wasn't enough, not when she was used to bathing in the creek. She still felt grimy, inside and out. And opening her door to see Beatrice standing in the hall, ramrod straight, did not appease the feeling.

"What do you want, Beatrice? Gabriel already told me he was sending me home." The word sounded alien on her tongue. Had she started to think of this awful place as home?

"I want to know why you changed out of your dress."

Something on Beatrice's face was—not anger. Not disdain. Something more...vulnerable. "You want to know what?"

"You put on that beautiful dress at the wedding and made sure everyone saw you, then you removed it. Why?"

Rebecca sagged against the door, too tired to hold herself upright against her sister-in-law's hatred. Again she decided on honesty. "I saw it was more elaborate than the occasion called for."

Beatrice pressed her lips together, almost appeased. "That was…considerate."

She turned away, not wanting Beatrice's approval any more than she wanted her disapproval. "The dresses aren't what I am any longer. Take what you think you can use."

Beatrice didn't say anything for a moment, before she burst out with, "But you're going home to San Francisco."

"It doesn't matter." She wouldn't be returning to the life she'd lived. She didn't know what, exactly, she would be returning to, but all the things she'd missed when she moved here were no longer important.

"I have sent Father a message that you are to return, and he has sent me your train ticket. You leave Friday," Gabriel announced over dinner two nights later.

Rebecca's bite of biscuit lodged in her throat. Two more days. But if Judah hadn't come back by now, he wasn't going to. She had never imagined he would be a man who would run away from his troubles. Who would leave without saying good-bye. He was more like Nathan than she thought. "Who will drive me?"

"I will."

That would be a joyful journey. She winced just thinking about it. "I'll be ready."

Down the table, Betsy sniffled. "I don't want Rebecca to go!"

David echoed the protest, and soon there were three crying children.

"Hush, now, we must make the best of our time together," Rebecca chided, though tears burned the backs of her own eyes. "You don't want me to remember you as soggy-eyed crybabies, do you? Finish your dinner and I'll take you to the creek."

"And tell us a story?"

"And tell you a story. But only if you stop crying."

But going to the creek didn't hold the same appeal. Rebecca only dangled her feet in the water as the children played.

The rattle of wheels on a rutted road carried over the valley, and she rose, drying her feet in her petticoats and beckoning the children to investigate. She shoved her damp feet in her boots and ushered the children in front of her as they hurried back to the house. She stopped short to see a carriage in front of the house, and Beatrice standing in the yard with her hand over her breast.

Neville Frost stood near the carriage door, and when he saw Rebecca, his expression brightened before collapsing into a frown. "Mrs. Chatham! How good it is to see you! I have been searching for you these long weeks." He crossed the yard to her in three long-legged strides and took her hand. "You look well."

But she could see the horror in his face at her plain appearance. Her own expression must echo his at finding him, the last person she would ever expect, here. And the disappointment that he wasn't Judah…

"I've come to take you back to San Francisco, where you belong."

"The gossip—"

"Has died down. I've come to offer you—"

She knew what he'd come to offer her, and held up a hand before he could say anything in front of the children. Her emotions tumbled over each other—shock, sorrow, and a hint of relief. She was going home Friday. Her father would set her out of the house. She would have no place to go. Unless she became Neville's mistress. Judah hadn't returned. She had no choice.

"Mrs. Chatham, are you not glad to see me?"

He was adorable, so young and needy, much like David. She offered him a smile. "I am indeed. Pardon my speechlessness. I never dreamed you would seek me out."

"I've come to rescue you," he said, throwing his shoulders back as he made the proclamation.

Her smile widened. Of course he would see it as such, as a knight in shining armor. "You are very sweet."

"Allow me to take you home."

But it wouldn't be home. It would be his home, and she would be his mistress, in his bed. She would lie with him and think of Judah. But what choice did she have? At the very least, he could take her to her father's house and she could face those consequences. Or he could take her to his home and she could forget all about Judah while she accepted Neville's attentions. She didn't know if she could shut off that part of herself.

"It's very late to make the drive back to Paso Robles," she said. "Perhaps my sister-in-law can find a place for you and your driver to bed down and we could make a fresh start in the morning." And she would have time to adjust to this new twist.

"Alas, I didn't know finding you would take so long, and we have return tickets on the morning train. My driver assures me we will be safe on the road back to the town, and we will stay in a hotel overnight. Where are your things? My driver will load them into the carriage." He stopped to take a breath. "My goodness, you are a sight for sore eyes, Mrs. Chatham." He took both her hands in his and smiled brightly. "Well. Shall we?"

"I don't have much." She turned away from him, seeing the disapproval on Beatrice's face as she walked past her.

"What are you doing?" Beatrice demanded, following Rebecca into her room.

"I'm leaving. That was the plan, wasn't it?"

"Not like this. Not in disgrace."

Rebecca straightened from folding up her other skirt. "Is that now how I was leaving? Is that not how I came here? That seems to be how I will live my life." While she had considered it before she came here, the idea now made her heart heavy.

"I thought you were in love with Mr. Merrill."

"Mr. Merrill seems to have disappeared, and I do not have time to wait on him. Nor do I want a man who runs from trouble. I had that before." She straightened and gripped the edge of her carpetbag. "Will you see that Mr. Frost has some refreshment as he waits? I do want to say goodbye to the children."

"Is that truly all you're taking with you?" Beatrice asked. "Now that you're returning to San Francisco, you'll need your finery."

"Mr. Frost will buy me new clothes."

"At what cost?"

True love, Rebecca thought, but didn't say.

———

San Francisco. Rebecca breathed in the cool crisp air of home, that now smelled so strange to her. Beside her in the carriage from the train station, Neville patted her hand.

"We'll get you situated at your apartment and then see about getting you some new gowns."

She nodded, because the lump in her throat wouldn't let her speak. He had been polite and solicitous on the carriage ride to Paso Robles, a much more comfortable journey in well-sprung conveyance, and traveling in the cool of the evening. Rebecca's thoughts hadn't calmed, however, and she'd cried when she said goodbye to the children.

Neville had arranged for separate hotel rooms when they arrived in Paso Robles after midnight, and bought them breakfast before they boarded the train. He'd ensured she and Sonia were comfortable on the ride back, and had been nothing but solicitous.

But soon he'd want her in his bed, and her heart ached. He wasn't Judah.

———

The next few days she was able to hold him off, pleading that her courses had come. She was overwhelmed by the generosity he'd shown her in the apartment he'd chosen, in the stylish part of downtown, with easy access to everything nearby. And she did love the city, and spent much of her day out in it, going into the shops and eateries with Sonia along. Sadly, though she had been given her own generous account, nothing particularly appealed.

Every afternoon, Neville escorted her to rides in the park. Last night they had gone to a play at the theater, and tonight they would go to a ball. She had seen people whispering behind their fans already. Everyone knew she was his mistress. She tried to remind herself that the woman she was before, after Nathan's death, would not have cared. But the woman who had fallen in love with Judah Merrill wanted to be worthy of his respect.

She dressed in the deep burgundy gown she'd bought the day after she arrived, knowing the tone set off her skin, and the silhouette favored her figure. Sonia arranged her hair in an elaborate style, with braids and curls. Rebecca knew she looked beautiful. But when she thought about why, she wanted to cry.

She let Sonia help her up from the chair in the dressing room that was bigger than Beatrice's kitchen, and went downstairs to meet Neville.

———

Judah stepped through the door of the grand home on Nob Hill, his hat in his hands. He'd done some quick talking to get into the ball, and was aware a butler or some other servant shadowed him as he overlooked the sea of people below. So many colors, so much opulence. Maybe he'd made a mistake coming here. Maybe this was where Rebecca belonged, among the riches and beauty. But no, he wasn't going to leave until he found her, and spoke with her, and Sonia said she was here.

Sonia had also assured him Rebecca had not been in this other man's bed. The entire journey north, that fear had twisted his gut, but he'd known it was possible and come anyway. Because he loved her.

And then he saw her. She was standing apart in a deep red gown that made the blue one she'd worn at the Raymonds' ranch look plain. Her hair was swept off her neck and the electric lights on the walls picked up the red highlights in her hair. She was alone, and she was sad.

Judah took the half-dozen steps down into the ballroom and crossed the glossy floor, aware his cheap black suit and skinny tie caused a ripple of remarks behind him. Drawn to the sound, Rebecca turned then and saw him. Her face drained of color and she swayed so that he reached out and grabbed her above the elbow. Her gloved hand gripped his forearm as her lips parted in shock.

"Judah, what are you doing here?"

Her appearance up close startled him. She was beautiful, yes, but exhaustion bracketed her eyes, which looked hollow and haunted. He moved closer, as if he could absorb some of her sorrow. "I've come to get you."

She released him and drew her arm out of his grasp, though it seemed she was reluctant to do so. "Have you?" Her tone was cool. "Have you come to rescue me as well?"

He frowned. "Rescue you? No. Is there a place we can talk?" People were beginning to stare at the fine lady talking to the cowboy.

She hesitated, then motioned toward the line of doors along one wall. "The terrace."

The terrace was just as busy as the ballroom, with couples coming and going from the overheated house, but at least it was quieter without the music and chatter that echoed off the walls. He moved closer, because he couldn't stay away.

"I shouldn't have left without letting you know where I was going."

Her chin came up. "No. you shouldn't have."

He turned his hat over in his hands, hoping those weren't tears glinting in her eyes. "I went to make arrangements. I've bought my land."

She met his gaze and gave him a small smile. "That's wonderful."

Her tone was warmer than her expression. "It isn't much right now, but I've got a shelter for the horses and I've spent the past three days building the crudest of lean-tos. I can do better, but I couldn't stay away a moment longer, and it seems my fears were well-founded. When I returned to your brother's, you'd already left for San Francisco." This wasn't going as he planned. He'd worked out beautiful things to tell her in his head, to get her to come home with him. Instead, he focused on the difficulties. "Life will be hard, no doubt, and more work than you are used to, but once we make our fortune, I promise this life can once again be yours."

Understanding crossed her face, and her lips parted. He feared she would protest, so he hurried on, taking her hand.

"I love you, Rebecca, though I fear I may be too late in my declaration."

Her posture stiffened. "Too late because now I am in another man's bed?"

The words hit him low and hard. "It doesn't matter to me."

"Of course it does. You're a man, and you're—good." She turned back to look over the gardens and flung her hand in his direction as if tossing an insult. "You of all people know why I am here."

"I know why." He touched her arm beneath her sleeve because he couldn't help himself. This time she didn't pull away. "And I know what I have to offer isn't as grand."

"Only love."

Her tone confused him. She said it like it was nothing, but her voice was choked. He gripped her arm and turned her toward him, pulled her close, ensuring she looked up into his face. "Only love. It's enough for me, Rebecca. Is it enough for you?"

"You there!" a man's voice called from the doorway to the ballroom, but Judah didn't turn, didn't take his gaze from Rebecca.

"Is it enough for you?" he repeated.

"You left me without saying a word," she said. "I would have waited for you if I had known you would return."

"It was a mistake. One I will never make again." He touched her hair, found it just as soft in the elaborate style that suited her, even as it didn't. "I promise you will know where I am every moment from now until the end of time."

A smile teased her lips. "I thought you were ashamed of me."

"Why would I be? You are the bravest woman I know."

The smile spread. "Then you must not know many."

Gaining confidence, he drew her closer so that her skirts brushed the tops of his boots and her hands flattened against his chest, over his heart. "You're the only one I need. Will you be my wife?"

"You there! Unhand her!"

She kept her gaze steady on his even as footsteps hurried in their direction. "Tell me why again."

"Because I love you. Because I want a life with you, as my partner, as my lover. It won't be a glamorous life for—"

She pressed her fingers over his lips. "Stop, before I change my mind. Yes, Judah. I will marry you." She rose on her toes and pressed her mouth to his.

Though she looked so different, she tasted the same, felt the same in his arms, sounded the same as she leaned into him. He folded his arms around her, San Francisco society fading away, everything he wanted here in his arms.

A hand clamped on his shoulder and he turned to see a very angry young man, flanked by three others.

"This is a private party. You need to leave."

Judah kept his arm wrapped securely around Rebecca's waist. "We shall."

The other man's hand shot out, blocking him, just inches from Judah's chest. "Alone. The lady is here with me."

"Not anymore," Rebecca said softly, breaking free of Judah's protective hold and moving to stand in front of him. She touched the young man's face and Judah's stomach clenched. "I'm sorry, Neville. Judah is my betrothed. We'll be leaving San Francisco. I thank you for all you've done for me, and I will find some way to repay you."

The anger left the young man's face as he looked down at her. "You can repay me by staying with me."

"I'm sorry," she said again. "But I don't love you. Now that I understand, I won't settle for less. You shouldn't, either." She rose on her toes and kissed Neville lightly on the mouth, then turned and took Judah's hand, her expression radiant. "Everyone deserves to find true love."

Together they walked down the stairs into the garden, away from the life she'd known, and into a life together.

Do you enjoy sexy western historical romances? Here's a sample of In the Marshal's Arms, a romance between a marshal and an outlaw's mistress.

Chapter One of In the Marshal's Arms

U.S. Marshal Rhys Burgess sat on his horse and looked down on the sad little ranch house below. It didn't look like much, certainly not like the home of one of the most ambitious bank robbers of the past decade.

The man he'd watched die last month.

The yard was barren, with a shriveled garden and unpainted house, barn, outhouse and chicken coop. No one was around, no hands, which made Rhys's plan easier, but made him wonder about the woman who worked this land on her own.

But the bank robber Edward Colby hadn't worked alone, and his brother was still at large. Rhys had heard Luke would come here, to the mistress he and his brother shared, to keep a low profile, and possibly bring some of the profits from their last job. And when he did, Rhys would be here waiting. He just had to convince Maddy Colby, the mistress who had taken the brothers' name.

He nudged his horse forward, down the hill.

A dog started barking frantically. Rhys scanned the yard, but saw nothing until the dog exploded from the house, stopping at the edge of the weathered porch and standing stiff-legged. The woman herself followed, a rifle in one hand, and shaded her eyes as she watched him approach.

Because she stood in the shadows, he didn't get a good look at her until he pulled Bathsheba up in the yard. When he did, she was nothing like he expected. Her dress was a plain worn calico day dress, and she was younger than he thought, not as tough as he would have thought the mistress of two outlaws would be. It looked like—did she have freckles?

"Help you?" she asked, lifting her hand to the auburn knot at the back of her head.

"I'm looking for work." He inclined his head toward the house. "Looks like you need some help around here."

She curved her shoulders forward in a defensive posture. "I don't have money to pay for help."

No money. It looked like she was telling the truth, but maybe it was just a plea for privacy. "Doesn't matter. I'll work for room and board. I been on the road a long time, ma'am, and I just need a place to stop for a bit."

She shifted the rifle into both hands. "You in trouble?"

He wondered if she knew how to use the gun. He was fairly certain Edward Colby would make sure of that. "No, ma'am."

She glanced behind her, but the intelligence he'd gathered in town already told him no one else was here. She was right to be wary, a woman alone out here.

"I'm not looking for help."

"What about protection?" He nodded at the mongrel. "I doubt he's a lot of good to you."

"I haven't had any trouble so far. All I need is for him to give me the alarm. I'm a fair shot." She lifted the rifle higher, as if planning to give him a demonstration.

"I believe that you are." He eased Bathsheba back just a bit, in case he had to bolt.

"My husband will be home soon."

He knew that wasn't true, but he decided to play along. Cautiously, he swung out of the saddle, facing her.

"He left you a lot of work here on your own. I could help you get it looking nice for when he returns. He'd appreciate that, don't you think?"

She lowered the rifle a bit, probably because it was growing heavy, and her eyelashes flicked. "How do I know you're a good guy?"

He wanted to tell her she should be able to tell a good guy from a bad guy after being involved with Edward and Luke Colby. Instead he said, "You don't. And I don't blame you for not taking my word for it. If it makes you feel better, I'll do some work for a meal and be on my way."

Her lips turned down and she lowered the rifle to her side. "You could do that. But I'll be watching you."

Relief ran through him and he patted his horse's neck. One day was a beginning. "You mind if I tend to Bathsheba first?"

"Go ahead." She gestured in the direction of the barn.

As he led his horse away, he wondered if she didn't get lonely out here, with only a dog for company. Honestly, he'd expected more of a fight.

A team of horses were the only occupants of the barn, which was in a sad state of disrepair. He unsaddled Bathsheba, rubbed her down, then gave her some grain, fed the team as well, and headed toward the house.

At the edge of the porch stood a curtained-off contraption with pipes and wooden posts, surrounded on three sides by muslin curtains. He peered inside to see the ground was moist. Above him hung something that looked like a giant watering can. He stepped back to see that the watering can was attached to a cistern.

"It's a shower," Maddy Colby said from the porch.

Rhys used every bit of training not to jump in surprise.

"When you need to cool off, or if you don't want to haul water for a bath, you bathe here." She approached warily, reached past him and tugged a rope. Water streamed out of the giant watering can in an even flow and splashed on the earth below.

"Your husband make that for you?"

"No, I did it," she said with some pride. "I have running water in my house, too."

He wasn't sure whether or not that was an invitation. "Sounds like a fine thing."

She nodded and he took a look at her in the sunlight. Her auburn hair was a myriad of colors—so many he wondered if two strands were the same. Her big brown eyes were long-lashed and her nose had a cute little slope, with a dusting of freckles. Pretty pink lips just begged for a man's kiss. Her dress was a faded calico, but it hugged her full breasts and nipped in at her narrow waist. He was surprised to see she was barefoot beneath her skirts.

How had an idiot like Colby won such a beauty?

"What would you like me to work on first?"

"I've been thinking on that," she said. "I've been trying to repair the roof, but it's a trick to climb around up there in a skirt."

He stepped back to look up at the angled roof. "I can see that. Where are the supplies?"

"Up there already, shingles, hammer and nails. The ladder's around back."

Indeed it was, already leaning against the edge of the house. And when he climbed up the steeply pitched roof to see she'd done a great deal of the work herself, he was impressed.

A few hours—and quite a few swear words later and a throbbing thumb later—Maddy Colby stepped out into the yard and shaded her eyes to look up at him.

"Mr. Burgess. Dinner will be ready in just a bit. Will you come down and take a shower?"

He set the hammer down and sat back on his heels. "I beg your pardon?"

"I—I don't want—just, before you come into the house."

"Ah." He did smell pretty bad, with trail dirt and sweat from being up here in the sun. Texas heat, even in November, could be a bitch. He'd thought about a bath, but he wondered about operating the shower. "Now?"

"Please."

He looked at the work he'd accomplished. Quite a lot but not done. He straightened, his back cricking, his shoulders aching. He hadn't done manual labor like this since he was a kid. He readjusted his hat and headed toward the ladder. When he looked down, she had gone inside.

Maddy stirred the gravy with a shaking hand. She hadn't had anyone to cook for in months and she enjoyed the process. She hoped Mr. Burgess had an appetite. In her experience, men did. She hadn't had any interaction with anyone in weeks, and hoped she remembered how without making too much of a fool of herself. She glanced out the front window and her spoon froze.

Mr. Burgess stood at the edge of the porch, close to the shower, and stripped off his undershirt, revealing a muscled chest and shoulders, a vee of black hair covering his chest, tapering down his flat stomach and into his pants. Her mouth went dry at the sight.

Edward Colby, her lover, had been a handsome man, fit, but barrel-chested and hirsute, and his brother Luke, who sometimes shared her bed, was broad-shoulders and heavily muscled. This man was lean, square-shouldered, the muscles in his arms and stomach flexing as he moved. He unbuckled his pants and her womanhood throbbed. It had been too long since she'd had sex. Edward had been killed and Luke hadn't returned for months. The brothers had taken her from the theater, where she'd had regular lovers between her nights on stage. The past few months were the longest she'd gone without a man, and Mr. Burgess was a fine specimen.

What would he think if she walked outside now? If she ran her hand down over his stomach and into his pants, curled her fingers around his cock?

Ridiculous woman. She knew nothing about this man. She

should have just had him move on, but she'd invited him on instinct. She did need help around the place. She needed to focus on that.

But those good intentions went to hell when he stripped off his britches. His cock lay heavy against the length of his thigh, and she could almost feel the weight of it in her mouth, the texture of it along her tongue. Sucking cock was one of her specialties. She enjoyed the act, the power it gave her. In her mind's eye, she could see Mr. Burgess's head fall back in pleasure when she knelt before him.

Mr. Burgess turned toward the shower, presenting her with his delicious backside, and fiddled with the rope. He tugged cautiously, then jumped back comically when the water splashed him. He edged toward the water, pulling the rope as he did so. Once he was fully in the shower, he released the rope and picked up the soap she'd left for him. She watched as he lathered his chest, then ran soapy fingers over his scalp, scrubbed his shoulders and thighs and groin. She wished he would allow her to scrub his back, just to feel his hard warm body. Her fingers curled against the window frame as he pulled the rope again and water sluiced over his body, slicking his hair back from his face, revealing strong bones there.

He stepped back onto the porch, picked up the drying sheet she'd left for him, and lifted his head.

She backed away from the window, hoping he hadn't seen her staring.

―――

Rhys rapped at the door of the cabin, feeling like a new man. A great contraption, that shower, better than sitting in a hip bath in his own filth. And after a day on the roof, he felt cool.

Mrs. Colby opened the door, a soft blush coloring her cheeks. She'd changed her dress, he thought. This one seemed to be darker, brought out her eyes. He looked past her to see two plates set on the table. The room itself was tiny, dominated by her bed. In addition to the two chairs at the table, another chair sat close to the stone fireplace on the opposite end from the kitchen, which was around the corner of the L-shaped house, and was just as small.

"It's been awhile since I cooked for someone other than myself," she murmured, opening the door wider. "I hope you're hungry."

"Famished." He stepped inside but felt uneasy about closing the door behind him. He was good at listening to his own instincts, and while he didn't think she was a danger to him physically, he was aware that an odd kind of energy heated the air.

"I'm a good cook, and I grow most everything myself." She removed the top from a large pot and steam rose, scented with pork. "I do need to go into town for some supplies. It's been awhile, but I think you'll enjoy it."

She served up green beans with chunks of pork, a chunk of meat that fell apart, it was so tender, and sliced up the lightest, airiest bread he'd ever seen. He slathered his piece with a hunk of butter as she watched, pride making her face glow.

"I'd thought your husband would have married you for your beauty," he said when he came up for air. "Now I see he married you for your cooking."

She gave a delighted laugh.

He motioned toward her still-empty plate. "You're not eating?"

"I wanted to make sure you had enough first. I was sure you'd have a large appetite."

Shamed at the way he'd plowed through the dinner, he set down his utensils. "I'm only making a glutton of myself, Mrs. Colby. My apologies for my bad manners."

"Not necessary. There is no greater compliment to a cook than to see a man dig in."

Though the taste of the food lingered and his mouth begged for more, he left his utensils on his plate and watched as she served herself tiny portions that wouldn't keep a bird alive. Frustrated, he took the spoon from her and doubled her portions. She laughed and began to eat.

"How long have you lived here?" he asked, cradling the cup of coffee between his hands as he sat back.

"Almost four years," she said.

"And before that? Where did you live?"

"I was born in the New Mexico Territory, and I worked there for a while before I joined a troop of actors and we moved from place to place before I met Edward."

He knew that, of course. "I imagine this life is quite different."

"It is quiet," she said with a wistful sigh. "But I enjoy having no one to answer to but myself."

"And your husband. Where has he gone?"

She shifted slightly in her chair and focused on her plate. "To Kansas to help his brother."

Kansas, where Rhys and several other marshals had learned about the bank robbery ahead of time, surrounded the bandits, and shot Edward Colby dead in the street. How much did Maddy know about his death? As much as he loathed the man and all he'd done, he didn't want Maddy to know the gruesome details.

"You said he'd be back soon?"

She concentrated on buttering a slice of bread. "He's been gone awhile."

For just a moment, he doubted that she knew of Edward's death, but no, he'd spoken to the marshal who'd delivered the news. Had she cried? Did she mourn him?

She looked up then. "What about you? Are you married?"

The question shouldn't have caught him off-guard, but it did. "My wife died a few years back." And he hadn't been able to bring himself to go home since. The life of a marshal had suited him as he grieved.

"No children?"

He shook his head. For that, at least, he could be grateful.

"No, we didn't, either. It's probably a blessing." Regret laced her voice.

He had to change the subject, and struggled for a topic to make her smile. "I should be able to finish the roof tomorrow," he said. "What do you have for me to do next?" Everywhere he looked, the place needed work, but he didn't know what her priorities were.

"The barn likely needs repair as well. I do need a trip into town, but I'm not sure about the state of the wagon."

"I'll take a look after dinner."

She pushed back from the table abruptly. "I made a pie."

That surprised a laugh from him. "You've been busy while I was on that roof."

"It's nice to have someone around to cook for. I usually just make bread for myself. I'm happy to remember I can cook."

Half an hour later, Rhys rose from the table, unable to remember the last time he'd eaten so much. His mother had been a good cook, but he'd left home seventeen years ago, and he'd had to share those meals with three brothers. His wife had been an adequate cook, but Mrs. Colby was clearly talented.

"I'm afraid I didn't leave much for you to put away for tomorrow," he said as she cleared the table.

"That's fine. If we can make it to town, I have no doubt I can make something to please you tomorrow."

"I'll go check on that wagon, then," he said. Best for him to leave this scene before it made him feel too domestic. He couldn't allow that.

Want to read more? You can find In the Marshal's Arms at all retailers.

About the Author

Emma Jay has been writing longer than she'd care to admit, using her endless string of celebrity crushes as inspiration for her heroes. Emma, married 35 years (wed at the age of 8, of course) believes writing romance is like falling in love, over and over again. Creating characters and love stories is an addiction she has no intention of breaking.

Also by Emma Jay

HISTORICALS

Eye of the Beholder

Wild Wild Widow

In the Marshal's Arms

Stealing the Marshal's Heart

CONTEMPORARIES

It Happened One Night series

One Crazy Night

One Rockin' Night

One Steamy Night

One Sizzling Night

One Wanton Night

Taming the Cowboy series

At the Cowboy's Mercy

The Cowboy's Saving Grace

Faith in the Cowboy

Bridesmaids in Paradise series

Her Perfect Getaway

Her Island Fantasy

Her Moonlit Gamble

Blackwolf Hot Shot series

All on the Line

Crossing the Line

Standing on the Line

Standalones

Riding Out the Storm

Two Step Temptation

Show Off

Off Limits

Lessons for Teacher

Two Nights on the Island

Hot and Bothered

Made in United States
Cleveland, OH
09 March 2025

could hardly form a coherent thought. Exhaustion dragged at her.

"Which trunk would you like in your room?" Mr. Merrill asked, his tone gentle, as if he understood.

But of course he didn't. "I'll have to go through them. Sonia packed them and I don't know what I have. Can't we leave them in the wagon until morning?"

"We have need of the wagon," Gabriel said sharply. "It was enough to do without it today."

Not having a choice, Rebecca forced herself not to stagger to the back of the wagon. With Sonia's help, she repacked her belongings, keeping her most practical items in the two carpetbags she'd brought along. She refused to acknowledge the sympathy in Mr. Merrill's eyes when he locked up her trunks and headed to the front of the wagon to deliver them to the barn. Instead she dragged herself into the house behind a triumphant Beatrice, ate a cold dinner of roast beef and potatoes, then followed Beatrice down a narrow hall to a tiny bedroom with two beds.

"We don't have a servants' quarters aside from the bunkhouse, and we were certain your maid wouldn't want to stay there, so she'll need to stay with you," Beatrice said. "Is there anything else you need?"

Her request for a bath seemed overwhelming. "Water to wash up with would be lovely."

"The well is out there." Beatrice pointed to a door in the hallway, leading out to the yard. "There's a bucket, but I've already put the fires out for the night, so cold water will have to do."

Cold water sounded wonderful after the heat of the day. Rebecca looked about. "A basin?"

Beatrice heaved a sigh, headed down the hall, and disappeared. Just when Rebecca thought she wouldn't return, she did, carrying a basin and a pitcher so small Rebecca would have to make several trips—or simply bathe by the well.

She chose the second. She stripped to her chemise and

marched out into the yard, swinging the basin in one hand and the pitcher in the other. She had used a well before, as a child, and lowered the bucket noisily, letting the pulley shriek and the bucket clatter against the stone sides. Let Beatrice be disturbed by the commotion.

Drawing the bucket up again took more strength than she expected, but she was too dirty and hot to give up now. For one horrible moment, she thought the bucket would overturn and spill the water back into the well, but with great effort, she managed to lift it over the side. After taking a healthy drink from the ladle, she lifted the bucket and poured the water down the front of her, plastering the chemise to her and raising goosebumps over her skin in the evening breeze. But, oh, it felt good enough to repeat, and she lowered the bucket, again making a racket and not caring. She repeated the process with the bucket, this time dumping it over her head. Her hair, already falling, tumbled past her shoulders with the added weight of the water, and the cool rivulets ran down her spine to the cleft of her bottom, over her throat, between her breasts.

Heaven.

As she lowered the bucket again, this time to fill the basin to take to Sonia, she noticed something that hadn't been there before, and she straightened to look into the amused eyes of Mr. Merrill.